'Why should

'Why shouldn't forward and reach balance herself.

His touch pierced ...kin with red-hot needles of desire, and shame at her reaction brought a wave of heat to her cheeks. She shook the hand away.

'Because I'm not as sophisticated, or civilised, or worldly as you!' she informed Jonathon angrily. 'And I see no reason for us to pretend to be something we're not!'

'We were friends before we were lovers, Meg.'

Having pursued many careers—from school-teaching to pig farming—with varying degrees of success and plenty of enjoyment, **Meredith Webber** seized on the arrival of a computer in her house as an excuse to turn to what had always been a secret urge—writing. As she had more doctors and nurses in the family than any other professional people, the medical romance seemed the way to go! Meredith lives on the Gold Coast of Queensland, with her husband and teenage son.

Recent titles by the same author:

COURTING DR GROVES

BY
MEREDITH WEBBER

MILLS & BOON

MILLS & BOON, the Rose Device and
LOVE ON CALL are trademarks of the publisher.
Harlequin Mills & Boon Limited,
Eton House, 18-24 Paradise Road, Richmond, Surrey TW9 1SR

© Meredith Webber 1996

ISBN 0 263 79537 3

*Set in Times 10 on 11½ pt. by
Rowland Phototypesetting Limited
Bury St Edmunds, Suffolk*

03-9604-47606

Made and printed in Great Britain

CHAPTER ONE

It was one of those lifts that emptied out through the back door, so those in the know did not walk in, then shuffle self-consciously around to face the front in the manner of normal lift-travellers. Instead, they filed neatly forward, presenting their anonymous, dark-suited backs to latecomers like Meg, who squeezed breathlessly between the closing doors.

And why the back of a stranger's neck, two rows in front of her, should activate her pulses, and start the twisting, angry pain again, she did not know. Although it had been the back of Jonathon's neck that had first attracted her—so different from all the other necks in the seats in front of her, necks with marks or scars, with straggly, unkempt hair.

Like this one, Jonathon's had been newly shaven, the hair recently trimmed. It was the precision of that hairline, the white band between it and the darkly tanned skin lower down the neck—a contradictory impression of vulnerability and strength—that had mesmerised her.

She realised with a startled wonder that she hadn't thought about him for weeks. Or was it months? She *must* be getting over him, after all, in spite of this unlikely and unwanted physical reaction to this stranger!

The head bobbed forward a little when the lift lurched to a halt, then disappeared as bodies surged outward, clotting for an instant in the slowly opening doors before spilling into a wide corridor.

Meg let them go, exiting more slowly as random images of the past played across her mind. Maybe it was the atmosphere of the court that had brought Jonathon to mind, although she hadn't given him a thought when she'd agreed to testify.

Her colleagues always grumbled when called as expert witnesses, but to Meg it was a new experience— and a release from the hectic grind at the hospital.

She had eagerly anticipated the break in routine; to breathing air that wasn't tainted with antiseptic, and to explaining the work she did. She had looked forward to experiencing a day in court, to seeing other professionals at work, and hearing a language that was unfamiliar in her ears. Now she wasn't so sure!

She shook off the darkness that had momentarily clouded her day of freedom—one neck wasn't going to spoil her 'holiday'!—and hurried down the corridor, following a sign that pointed towards Court Four.

'Dr Groves!'

The voice made her turn. Peter Watson, the prosecuting attorney, was waving a sheaf of papers as he tried to attract her attention.

'I wanted to run through the procedure with you,' he said, uncharacteristically using words that were familiar after all! 'You'll be asked to wait outside the courtroom until you're required. At the moment you're listed as the second witness of the morning, so it shouldn't be too long a wait—provided the defence doesn't want to argue points of law or bring up something with the judge.'

'I assume someone will tell me when I'm on,' Meg responded with a slight smile. Peter was always so earnest, so meticulous in his explanations. He reminded her of a small boy reciting his lessons.

Now he nodded in reply to her question, but didn't return the smile.

'A court officer will come out. He or she will lead you to the witness stand, the bailiff will swear you in, then I'll stand up and ask the questions we discussed last week.'

'And I answer simply and clearly, looking at the jury so I can make certain they're following what I'm saying.'

Again Peter nodded, but this time he added the smile. 'You can't think how good it is to deal with someone who actually understands what we're trying to do,' he told her, admiration clear in his brown eyes.

A commotion further down the corridor drew their attention.

'I think that means I'm wanted,' Peter told her. 'There are chairs outside the door where you can sit. We haven't talked about cross-examination, but it's the same procedure as my questioning. The defence chap will ask you questions—if he thinks there's a point he might raise. All you have to do is answer him the same way you answer me. With any luck, he won't bother!'

Another smile, a reassuring pat, and he was gone.

'Leaving me far more apprehensive than I was when I arrived,' Meg muttered to herself.

She continued down the now deserted corridor, wondering if the patients she reassured before operations were left with a similar uneasiness. Did oversimplifying what was about to happen destroy confidence, rather than enhance it? She settled stiffly on the hard-backed chair and her mind bit into the problem, pleased to have something to divert it from the unknown that lay ahead.

'Dr Groves!'

A young policewoman peered through the opened door of Court Four. Meg felt her stomach clench then somersault, and silently chided herself for reacting so fearfully.

Not quite the cool, contained, super-confident specialist you like to pretend you are! her cynical mind mocked as she rose to her feet and followed the young woman into the court-room.

The neck was there—that was the first thing she noticed! Bent over a table on the left of the court-room, furthest from the witness stand.

She glanced around the rest of the room, sorting out the layout in her mind. It was surprisingly restful.

The trappings of justice, made familiar by television dramas—jury box, witness stand, bench and tables— were fine pieces of furniture, fashioned from a pale, evenly grained wood.

The judge looked properly solemn, and that man at the desk in front of him would be his clerk. The woman in the dark suit walking towards her would be the bailiff—neatly efficient! To one side of the bench, a stenographer sat with fingers poised above a small machine.

Peter smiled encouragingly, and she made it to her appointed place without falling over her feet.

As she repeated the oath she looked at the jury— seven men and five women—all watching her with a wariness that puzzled her, until she realised that they were probably as new to this court formality as she was. Did they want to be here? Were they interested, or resentful? The questions jostled in her head.

Look at the jury when you speak, she reminded herself as Peter walked towards her. She kept her eyes on him, breathing deeply while she steadied herself, and thought of the injury she would have to describe.

Her name and qualifications safely over, she ventured a glance at the judge. He was watching her with polite attention, but beyond him an overweight man in the jury box was shifting uneasily in his chair. Was he bored already? Would he listen to what she had to say? He was the one she would have to convince, she decided, and the thought of this challenge cleared her mind, and stiffened her resolution.

'Now, Doctor, could you tell the court where you were on the evening of the twenty-fourth of May last year?' Peter began.

'I was on duty at the Shorehaven Hospital.'

'In the casualty ward?'

'No.' Meg turned slightly, so she could look directly at the fidgety juror. 'As orthopaedic registrar, I was on call to all parts of the hospital, although, at night, most of my work came from Casualty and the accident and emergency rooms. That night there had been a car accident at about ten o'clock, and I had been in the operating theatre for three hours before the call came through that I was needed in Casualty.'

Peter smiled slightly and she knew she had passed the first test. All too often, he had told her, expert witnesses used the abbreviations of their trade. Unfamiliar verbal shorthand like 'Cas' or 'A and E' could have put some jury members off balance from the beginning.

With a patience that was a lesson in itself, he took her through the incidents as they had occurred that evening, from the time she had been called down to

Casualty to speak to the doctor treating the man with
the bleeding knife wound.

Careful not to upset the jury with an excess of blood,
or technicalities beyond their grasp, Meg explained
that the knife had entered the patient's wrist, severing
the median nerve and two flexor tendons, and opening
the radial artery.

'And what would such an injury mean in the long
term?' Peter asked.

'The tendons control the movement of the wrist,
some run through the superficial flexor compartment
to the palm of the hand, while the median nerve carries
the messages that control sensation and movement in
the fingers.'

She paused for a moment and flexed her hand, and
was pleased to see several members of the jury imitate
her action. 'The damage to the artery meant there was
a lot of blood about, and the severed nerve meant the
patient had lost feeling in his fingers, but the total
division of the tendons required the most urgent
action.'

Led by Peter, she described the microsurgery she
had performed, gathering confidence as she spoke of
the familiar operation.

'And was this surgery carried out immediately?'
Peter asked.

She nodded, then remembered the briefing. The
court stenographers could not record nods!

'It was performed within an hour of the patient's
being admitted.'

'You performed this operation at two o'clock in the
morning, after three hours in the operating theatre
patching up the road-accident victims?' Peter's voice
had a subtle shading of incredulity. 'Is this routine

procedure? Wouldn't such a small wound normally have been stitched in Casualty? Or, if surgery was required, couldn't it have waited until morning, when there was a full complement of surgical staff on duty?'

Meg heard a suggestion of excitement in Peter's voice now, and recognised it as the thrill of the chase. In the same way as she would follow the course of a microscopic blood vessel in search of a tear she knew must be there, he had tracked the course of her testimony, heading unerringly towards this one point.

'Urgent surgery is always indicated if flexor or extensor tendons in the wrist, hand or fingers have been severed, or are suspected to have been severed,' she replied carefully, hoping that the jury remembered her explanation of flexion and extension.

'And why is it so urgent?' Peter asked the question calmly but winked so that only she could see his delight.

'Because the cut ends of the tendon, particularly on the body side of the injury, may retract—shrink back—to such an extent that it is difficult, and sometimes impossible, for a surgeon to repair it later.'

'And if it is not repaired?'

'It would result in contracture of the joint, and permanent disability.'

Meg bent her wrist forward to illustrate the position of a contracted wrist, and looked directly at the overweight jury man. He had stopped shuffling in his seat and appeared to be interested in her explanation.

'A permanent disability?' Peter queried, patent disbelief colouring his voice. 'From a simple knife wound that left a scar of less than an inch?'

'If it had not been treated promptly,' Meg confirmed as sweet relief flowed through her body.

She had done it! She had answered the questions and got across the one message Peter wanted to instil in the minds of the jurors, and without a single interruption, without one call of 'Objection' from the opposition.

Maybe that only happened in films and television shows, she thought, turning for the first time to look at the people at the defence table—at the man or woman who hadn't cried 'Objection!'.

Objection! Objection! Objection!

The word hammered in her skull. Directly in front of her, Peter was saying something to the judge, but his form was a shadowy, unfocused blur. Her gaze was fixed on the man rising to his feet behind the far table; the man with a silly grey wig hiding the newly cut hair, concealing the light brown colour, and the lighter, sun-streaked tips that she knew would be splashed through it.

She gripped the front of the stand, forcing her body to remain upright, while her heart hammered, her knees wobbled, and her temperature fluctuated so rapidly that her hands grew damp while her body shivered.

'. . .still on oath, Dr Groves.'

The judge rose to his feet, nodded to the jury, who were rising stiffly from their chairs, and left the court-room.

'He's leaving the cross-examination until after lunch,' Peter explained. 'Are you OK?'

He was peering anxiously at her, the triumphant delight she had seen earlier on his face wiped away by concern.

'I'm fine,' she muttered. 'Maybe suffering a little from reaction.'

She risked one quick glance at the defence table. The man in the wig and his two cohorts were shuffling papers. Of course it was Jonathon! Her mind refused to argue logically, to accept that Jonathon was ten thousand miles away—practising law, it was true—and not here in the southern Queensland town of Shorehaven.

'That's natural!' Peter responded with a false heartiness that grated on Meg's nerves. 'Come on, I'll buy you lunch.'

He took her arm as she stepped down from the witness box.

It's a man who looks like him, she told herself, allowing Peter to lead her towards the door. But her body told her differently, and, as she passed closer to the table, she looked again.

Clear green eyes, so full of hunger that they seemed to burn into her soul, met hers for an instant. Then, as an answering desire flared through her with a savagery that clawed at her stomach and tore at her throat, she saw the need change to anger, and his head turn deliberately away.

Pain quenched the fires! Not a lift of an eyebrow, a nod of acknowledgement! She stumbled along beside Peter, grateful for his guiding hand as hurt and confusion blinded her.

Could Jonathon hate her so much? But he was the one who had brought an end to their relationship, the one who had decided to go back to England to finish his law degree.

The anger stunned him! Dark and hot, pulsing through his body like some demonic fury. It was because she was so thin. In some deep recess of his mind he recognised that. Thin, and tired, and pale—an insubstantial wraith drifting through the world, set apart from its chaos and its pleasures. Or did she still come back to vibrant life in the ether-studded air of the operating theatre or the antiseptic-laden corridors of the hospital?

She had always driven herself to the limit of her endurance—compulsively seeking not success, but perfection. His lips twisted at the thought, a bitter, rueful parody of a grin.

No, that hadn't changed. He'd seen her glance swiftly around the room as she had come in, but after that her whole being had been concentrated on the judge and jury, her responses so clear and concise that a child could have followed what she was saying.

Her total preoccupation had given him time to study her, to try to sum up dispassionately just what it was about his relationship with Megan Groves that had affected his life so badly. Long ago she had refused to give him the commitment he'd wanted, but since that time he had been unable to offer permanence in any relationship.

She was thinner than he remembered, but, to him, still damnably attractive. Yet he met a dozen more beautiful women each year. He had looked again, taking in the tall, slim figure standing erect in the witness box. She was arresting! That was the word, he had decided, seeing the clean lines of her classical profile, the shadows beneath her high cheekbones, and the full, wide lips which were so reluctant to smile.

Remembering that slow transformation of her face, from serious to wryly amused, had sent sparks shooting through his blood. Dispassionate appraisal! he had reminded himself.

Her hair was short now, straight and shiny, like a little cap on the top of her elegant head. He should be disappointed, because, in his fantasies, they were always in bed, and long strands of hair lay across her white, white skin like arrows, leading his lips on and on. . .

'. . .tough nut to crack.' The defence solicitor was talking to him, but the words made little sense to Jonathon. He was too busy trying to analyse his reactions.

In his mind—during sleepless nights, or in futile daydreams—he had imagined their next meeting. He'd considered some reserve would be inevitable, an initial awkwardness, some tenderness perhaps. He'd envisaged pain, uncertainty. What he hadn't considered was the fierce, searing heat of desire that had swept up from his loins, or the all-consuming anger that had followed it!

He turned to the solicitor and made some meaningless reply.

Could two people whose lives had once resembled a permanent state of spontaneous combustion simply walk past each other like that, Meg wondered dazedly, not even acknowledging the other's presence with a nod?

Disappointment doused the last tremblings of excitement in her bones, and killed the final flickerings of shock along her nerves. Doors opened and closed, the lift moved downwards, and she wrapped her arms around her shoulders, hunching protectively forward.

Her body felt as cold as death itself, her heart as solidly unresponsive as the granite plinths that flanked the courthouse doors.

'The barrister for the defence is an English chap,
although I believe he studied here,' Peter told her,
steering her through the vestibule, and out into the
sunshine.

Should I say I know that? Meg wondered, but the
decision was postponed. Peter was speaking again
before she could force her numb lips into motion.

'He's working in Brisbane. Only been back in
Australia for a few weeks, from what I can gather, so
he's an unknown quantity.'

They came to a halt at the kerb, waiting for a car
to pass.

'Does it matter?' Meg asked. 'Surely there are only
so many questions the defence can ask, especially with
technical evidence? Facts are facts,' she added, trying
to calm her inner agitation with a common-sense discussion. 'No amount of clever questioning can
alter them.'

Sensing movement behind her as other people
trickled out of the court building, she stepped down
on to the road, and, evading Peter's restraining hand,
dodged between two approaching cars, and made the
safety of the other side.

'Do you always cross roads like that?' he asked
breathlessly when he caught up with her on the other
side. 'And I thought we'd go to Mirabelle for lunch—
it's back this way.'

'We've got an hour and a half, and a walk will do
us both good,' Meg declared, striding onward as if a
pack of demons was on her heels. 'We can eat at the
hospital canteen—at least there we'll be away from
any legal spies!'

If she hadn't been in such a panic to get away
as fast as she could, she would have laughed at

Peter's outraged expression. Fancy restaurants and expense-account lunches were more Peter's style than canteen food! But escape was uppermost in her mind, and her back tingled with reminders of Jonathon's proximity.

Peter shrugged, then, accepting the inevitable, fell into step beside her, reverting back to her earlier comment.

'Facts might be facts but they can be interpreted in different ways, coloured by nuances, or distorted by a particular emphasis. Top barristers demand huge fees because of their ability to project the facts to the jury in such a way that their client is shown in the best possible light.'

Meg nodded her understanding. 'It's the same with surgeons,' she agreed. 'Any half-trained student could suture up a skin wound, but, if you want invisible mending, you pay for the best.'

But Jonathon's an unknown quantity, she argued silently. Why him? Unless. . .

The thought brought back the shivery feeling, and she quickened her pace, seeking escape, not from his physical presence, but from her own unwelcome suspicions.

'They wouldn't be paying much for such a newcomer,' Peter reassured her. 'Although it's strange a local firm of solicitors would go to Brisbane for a barrister.'

His words confirmed her worst fears. Someone in the solicitor's office knew of Jonathon's medical training. Not so strange, since he had completed his medical degree in Brisbane before reverting to law. And students of the time would remember his father, who had come from England to take up the position of vice-chancellor at the university, bringing with him his student son. . .

Memories battered at the walls she'd erected around them in her mind, but she held firm against their demands, knowing that, if one or two trickled through, a flood would follow.

Would Jonathon's medical knowledge matter? Would he be able to alter the facts because of his specialised experience? She made herself think of possibilities, to anticipate what he might ask that would shade or colour the facts she had presented to the jury, but her mind wouldn't concentrate on practical matters. It kept asking why! Why had he come back to Australia? Why Brisbane? Why hadn't he contacted her? Why should he?

The last question stopped her in her tracks. There was no reason why he should have. Whatever had been between them was over long ago—finished. Dead as any proverbial dodo. Which was how she wanted it!

'If you insist on eating at this place, you might at least lead the way to where the food is!' Peter grumbled.

Meg looked vaguely around, and realised she was propped in the middle of the hospital foyer. All about her, people moved purposefully, their swift progression a choreography of efficiency and competence.

'It's this way,' she muttered, battling against her bewildering thoughts. Seeing Jonathon had awoken the dreadful physical yearning she thought had died long ago, but she was older and wiser now. Surely she had learned that a physical relationship, no matter how wildly, ecstatically and splendidly fulfilling, was not enough?

She had lived through the initial agony of his departure, had learned to hide the pain, and smother the longing. There was no way she was going to go through all that again!

Moving mechanically, she grasped a tray, then pushed it along the rack beneath the self-service food counter. Plastic-wrapped sandwiches landed on it, followed by a small bottle of apple juice, a piece of cake. It was as if her hands were working independently of her mind, procuring the food her body needed to keep functioning.

'Coffee?' Peter asked, and she nodded, then watched him pay for both the lunches. She was beyond arguing equal rights, beyond any rational thought. What she really wanted to do was go home to her little flat, climb into bed and pull the covers over her head, in the futile hope that reality might turn into a dream.

'If I were acting for the defence,' Peter said, when they were settled on the uncomfortable plastic chairs in the courtyard beyond the canteen, 'I would concentrate on the medical aspect. The woman has admitted she stabbed her husband, so the best the defence can hope for is getting a conviction of unlawful injury.'

Meg nodded. Peter had explained this before. Unlawful injury covered most minor assaults, and drew a less severe penalty than the more serious charge of grievous bodily harm.

'Would she go to jail for either of those charges?' she asked, surprising herself. It was the first time she had considered 'the accused' as a person, or wondered what might be the outcome of the case. Until this minute she had not thought beyond delivering her evidence!

The realisation stunned her. Was she so far removed from people that the woman's plight did not affect her either way? Had she withdrawn so far into her own restricted, blinkered world that she could be unaffected by any other aspect of this case? That she had not bothered to ask why the woman had stabbed her husband? Nor wondered what had provoked enough fury to drive a jewelled silver letter-opener through his wrist?

The policewoman on duty as a court officer welcomed her back after lunch, motioning her back to the witness stand. Meg sat down, dreading the moment when she would have to face Jonathon across the pale timber railing.

Think of something else, she ordered her disoriented brain.

Her lunchtime speculation made her look at the woman they called 'the accused' for the first time. She was beautiful—blonde, petite, yet exquisitely proportioned. Meg was sorry she hadn't asked Peter more about the case, sorry she had been so focused on her own small part in it that she had failed to find out exactly what had happened, and why.

The husband, she remembered, had been solidly built, with an air of authority that came from more than wealth. As a patient, he had been quiet and polite, submitting to her ministrations with a tight-lipped composure. Again she wondered what had happened between them—and how much hatred must have built up for him to proceed with criminal charges against the lovely woman he must once have loved.

But she knew how love could hurt the loved one. . .

Doors opened, the jury sorted themselves into their correct seats, lawyers reappeared, then everyone rose. The judge was back.

Look at him or the jury, Meg reminded herself, but her skin knew Jonathon was approaching, moving easily towards the witness box.

Now the pale timber witness box became a prison, and she slid her hands down to her sides, and gripped the edges of the chair to stop herself from trembling.

He greeted her politely, stranger to stranger, his eyes encouragingly friendly—and totally impersonal. She was a witness he wished to use—to question and confuse as much as possible. Someone it was his job to discredit!

The enormity of the situation shuddered through her. Would he take pleasure in the task? She didn't know, and that upset her more than anything. Once she had known all his thoughts—or thought she had!

'You have explained, most concisely, the injuries your patient suffered, Dr Groves,' he began, 'but left us with few impressions of your patient as a person, or your own reaction to the injury.'

He smiled—the charming, whimsical smile that had once turned her world upside-down. Now it filled her with pain and apprehension. He half turned, so he faced the judge and jury, before speaking again.

'Perhaps you could tell us what happened when you met your patient on that night. What explanation he offered for the wound. How he seemed to you. Was he upset? Flustered? Angry?'

Meg drew a deep breath. Would her voice shake when she tried to use it? Would she stutter and stammer, revealing the inner turmoil that churned through her body?

'Mr Staines was admitted by the resident on duty in Casualty,' she said carefully. 'The details of how the injury occurred would have been given to him.'

'And written on his file, surely?' Jonathon prompted without turning back to her. She looked at the straight, clean profile, at the crease down his cheek that puckered into a dimple when he smiled—and hated him. It had been an old debate between them—this subject of which was more important, the person or the condition? Once she had enjoyed arguing with him, batting the subject back and forth, calling up arguments to support her ideas!

She took a deep, steadying breath and replied carefully, 'I was asked to look at the injury, to assess the extent of the damage, and to decide what should be done.'

'And the man's mental state or the cause of the injury had nothing to do with you?'

It wasn't exactly a sneer, but it was close enough to start a slow burn of anger deep within her.

I'm an orthopaedic surgeon, not a psychiatrist, she wanted to shout, but caution prevailed. That was exactly what Jonathon wanted her to do.

'I was called from the operating theatre to see this patient, and had a child waiting upstairs for her ankle to be set. I examined the wound, explained to the patient that it should be operated on immediately, and made arrangements for pre-operative blood tests to be done and a drip started.'

'You didn't answer my question, Doctor!' Now he turned towards her, and this time he didn't smile. For an instant she thought she saw a flash of pity in his eyes. 'Did your patient's mental state warrant no consideration at all?'

With a calm deliberation, she directed her words towards the jury. 'Mr Staines was rational, calm and composed,' she said coldly, ignoring the man who stood so close—denying the silent messages bombarding her body.

'Exactly how you'd expect a man to be when his wife had attacked him and plunged a silver dagger through his wrist?'

It was a teaser, tempting her towards some trap his tortuous mind was preparing for her. Was it a question? Did she have to answer?

She glanced at the judge, who had his head cocked enquiringly to one side.

'He was calm and composed,' she repeated.

'So calm and composed that you didn't ask how the injury had occurred?'

'How it occurred was not my problem,' she replied, crisply dismissive of his persistence. The startled look on the jurors' faces told her she had stepped unwarily. Did she seem cold and clinical to them? Was that the image he was trying to project?

'Not even if he had plunged the dagger through his arm himself? If he had snatched it from his wife, and ripped it into his own flesh?'

The questions must have been rhetorical, for he continued speaking without pausing to draw breath.

'During your training, and subsequent years of practice, how many open-wrist injuries have you seen?'

Meg was puzzled, but relieved by the change of attack. She answered quickly, 'Probably twenty-five or thirty.'

'Twenty-five or thirty slashed wrists!'

As soon as he spoke she saw that he hadn't changed direction, but simply honed in on another possible weakness. She found herself stiffening as he plucked away at her straining nerves with his insinuations, and her mind began to spin as she tried to work out how she could regain the lost ground.

'Isn't it true that most injuries of this kind are self-inflicted, Dr Groves?' he murmured, the soft words clear enough to carry to the jury.

'This was a puncture wound, such as can result from falling onto a sharp object, or stabbing a sharp object through the skin. Self-inflicted wounds are usually longer and more shallow—slashes, if you like the word!'

'So you didn't consider the possibility of attempted suicide when you saw the wound?'

The woman has admitted she ran at him with the knife, Meg thought, thoroughly confused by the strange twists and turns in Jonathon's questioning. She glanced across at Peter, but his gloomy face offered little help.

'No, I didn't,' she told him. 'I considered only what had to be done to prevent—' she tried to remember what Peter had told her about the two charges. Unlawful wounding meant a break in the skin and bleeding, while grievous bodily harm meant permanent damage without medical intervention '—his being maimed for life.'

She felt a surge of triumph. Surely that was the way to answer, repeating words Peter wanted the jury to remember?

'But if he was suicidal a maimed hand would matter little to a corpse,' Jonathon objected. 'Did you not consider you had some duty or responsibility to check the man's mental state?'

Her own momentary relief was swept away by Jonathon's voice, so cold and clear—so condemning!

She heard Peter object, heard the judge rule out the question, but time slipped sideways as the same accusing voice came echoing from the past.

CHAPTER TWO

'How a woman who is as fiery and tempestuous, as uninhibited and generous, as passionate and provocative as you are in bed can be so detached from human emotion in your everyday life, is beyond me!'

Jonathon had yelled the words at her, torn from his usual composure by the enormity of whatever sin she had committed. Meg couldn't remember what had triggered the outburst, but the condemnation had followed her through the years, reminding her that to show too much of herself to anyone was to invite pain.

'You must answer the question!'

The judge's deep voice brought her back to the present, and she turned to Jonathon, her eyes blurred by the transient memories.

'I asked if, in your opinion, the wound could have been self-inflicted?' Jonathon growled, patience and control flying out of the window as he looked into her soft brown eyes. She had that dazed look he had only ever seen after they had made love. As if, for some short space of time, she'd been transported to another realm beyond reality, and was now having trouble finding her way back to earth.

'I suppose it's possible,' she muttered.

For an instant, her eyes clung to his as they had long ago. Desperate and appealing, begging him to guide her back to the real world; to help her make sense of the enormity of her passion. Back then he'd held her tight, whispering sweet, silly nothings into her

25

ear, smoothing her hair, kneading her flesh, until the soul he only glimpsed in the shadows of those dark eyes returned to her body, and the cool, controlled, work-driven Meg replaced his magical, wanton Meggie.

And he'd fooled himself into thinking she needed him!

'You suppose it's possible.' He bit the words out, as long-buried resentment threatened to destroy his composure and make him lose control of this case. He ignored the quick flash of shock in her eyes, and the mute appeal that followed it, and repeated the words in his most derisive court-room voice. 'You suppose it's possible!'

He turned away from her pale face, and spread his hands wide towards the jury.

'I have no further questions of this witness, Your Honour,' he said grimly, and walked back to his chair.

There were voices, then someone said, 'You may step down, Dr Groves,' and she moved, although her body felt as numb as her mind.

He had discredited her! Jonathon, whom she had loved with every cell of her body, had stripped away her credibility in front of all those people, and then turned his back on her, leaving her defenceless—and more alone than she had ever felt in her life.

Chris Wells, the prosecution's instructing solicitor, caught up with her as she pushed through the heavy door. He followed her out into the corridor.

'But the woman admitted stabbing him, didn't she?' she pleaded, hoping Chris might deny this. Then she could believe Jonathon's attack had been to put doubt into the jury's mind; to make them wonder if the husband, not the wife, had caused the wound.

'Of course she has,' Chris said bracingly, killing the hope stone-dead. 'He's a clever blighter, though, bringing up the possibility of a suicide attempt to make the issue seem less clear. If the jury starts to think about that, no matter how irrelevant it is, it pushes your evidence further back in their minds, makes it less meaningful. Can I get you a cab?'

He sounded so matter-of-fact that she looked at him more closely. Did he not care if the case went against him?

Meg shook her head. She would walk back up to the hospital—go back to work. Her 'holiday' mood was shattered, and she longed for the security of that bustling, walled-off, private world she had made her own.

'I thought you'd taken the whole day off,' Janet Greene chided when she appeared in the fourth-floor orthopeadic ward. 'Not that we're not glad to see you. Bed Five—the broken leg—is in a lot of pain.'

Meg winced inwardly at Janet's reference to a patient as a bed number, but the ward sister was speaking again, so she did not make her usual protest.

'We've elevated the leg, and I've been doing four-hourly neurovascular checks, but I didn't like to do anything else until a doctor saw him. I called for Bill, but he's in Theatre at the moment.'

'I'll see Mr Rogers now,' Meg assured her, and walked away, but the conversation—so typical that it was repeated countless times each week—stayed with her. Janet was a super-efficient nurse, much-loved by all her patients, so did it matter that she called Mr Rogers 'Bed Five'?

And did she, Meg, care more for Mr Rogers because she called him by his name? She shook her head, depressed by where her thoughts were leading. Janet probably had more caring and compassion in her big toe than she had in her whole body, she decided gloomily. At least, that was the way it had seemed lately.

She crossed to the bed, and smiled warmly at the 'broken leg'. Mr Rogers' tentative response told her the smile had not been expected. The poor man seemed almost shocked by it, although she had been the doctor treating him for the past four days.

'Sister tells me you're in pain,' she said gently, reaching out to feel the toes that protruded from the long leg cast. They were colder than she would have expected.

'It's round the ankle, Doctor,' Mr Rogers said. 'A burning kind of pain.'

'Is it better since Sister raised your leg?' Meg picked up his chart from the foot of the bed, but instead of reading the new notations while she waited for his reply she watched his face, and saw him thinking about the question and how to frame his reply so she might understand.

Do I remove or distance myself from people? And does that destroy some of my effectiveness as a doctor? Questions she had not asked herself for years now nagged in her mind, put there by the dark shadow of the past.

'It's not much better,' Mr Rogers declared after considerable consideration. 'Might be a bit, but not much!'

'Is it the inside or the outside of your ankle?' Meg asked, switching her mind firmly back to practicalities.

Her patient leaned awkwardly forward, using one hand to indicate the area of distress. If the plaster was rubbing on his ankle, would the pain be localised there, or seem to come from all around the joint?

She thought about it for a moment, then looked up to see him looking anxiously at her. She smiled again. Two smiles in one consultation! she taunted herself silently, but his anxiety remained fixed in her mind.

'I could cut a "window" in the plaster,' she told him. 'Take out a bit and have a look around. If the plaster is rubbing on the skin, or pressing on the bone, it would explain why it's so painful.'

Mr Rogers nodded. 'Then you'd leave it open so it doesn't rub again?' he offered, and she had to shake her head.

'If we leave it open then the tissue in the uncovered area will swell out into the space, and you'll end up in all sorts of trouble. When we cut a window we strap the piece we cut out back in place with elastic tape, but we can undo it whenever we like to have a look at what's happening in there.'

'So they let you go free!'

Meg spun around as the cheerful voice boomed in her ear. Bill Jackson, the orthopaedic resident, was bearing down on her, reminding her, as always, of an over-large but amiable St Bernard.

'And you've beaten me to Mr Rogers' little problem. I thought this was one I was going to be able to sort out on my own.'

'Go right ahead,' Meg retorted, waving her hand towards their patient. 'I'm certain Mr Rogers will agree that two heads are better than one. I've explained that we could "window" the cast, but that's as far as I've got.'

Ignoring the startled expression in Bill's eyes, she moved around the bed and sank down into the visitor's chair. Bill was on the orthopaedic programme to learn the intricacies of the specialty—maybe it was time she let him take more responsibility.

She watched him reach out to touch the patient. He was surprisingly gentle for such a large man. His hands moved deftly, and he repeated the questions Meg had asked.

'There could be swelling in the lower leg. I'd take it off the cast, slit it both sides, and bi-valve it.'

Third smile! Meg felt it twitch across her lips.

'I agree,' she said. 'There's no point in peering through a window if the trouble is somewhere else. If Mr Rogers was going home and would be weight-bearing immediately, I'd hesitate, but, as he's here with us for another week, I think we'll cut it, and have a look, then replace it using bandages to hold it together.'

She paused and looked at Bill. 'Are you finished in Theatre? Would you like to do it?'

Her strange mood threatened to tilt back to her normal repressiveness when she saw the quick frown on his face. It was as if she had never offered to let him do anything for her patients in the four months he'd been here! The thought shocked her. Was she becoming so absorbed in her work that she no longer considered other people's needs and feelings? Had she turned into the super-efficient machine Jonathon had warned she could become?

'Well?' she asked again.

'Sure would!'

He grinned at her with such open delight that she had to smile back, then she nodded at him and walked away, calling over her shoulder, 'And you'd better do a good job—I could sneak back to check your handiwork later!'

She heard their chuckles following her, and some of

the torment in her heart eased. It was because she'd been so busy lately, had had so little time for individual patients. . .

She crossed the corridor, lost in thought, and entered one of the single-bed rooms on the other side. Gemma was sleeping, her slight form a fragile wisp beneath the covering sheet. Meg crossed to the chair and sat beside her, one hand reaching out to brush a strand of lint-fair hair from the pale cheek.

A nurse popped her head around the door. 'She's been cheerful and bright today!'

Meg nodded. Gemma was well enough to be discharged. After four months, and countless operations, the little girl could finally go home—if she had a home to go to.

Her heart squeezed painfully.

Behind her, the door opened, and Mark Reynolds, the patient-welfare officer, came quietly into the room, accompanied by a woman who could only be another government official. Welfare, not police, Meg decided. So far, all the people who had come and peered at Gemma had looked the same—caring and concerned, but harassed by the problem of 'placing' her. To Meg, the word 'placement' was an affront, although she could not have explained why.

She stood up and walked across to the door, so they could speak without disturbing the sleeping child.

'No one positive has turned up in response to the photos we printed in the interstate newspapers,' Mark murmured to her. 'It's been a month now.'

'Photos?' the stranger asked. 'You put photos of the child in newspapers?' She sounded horrified. 'It's up to the police and the children's services department to do that. Who knows what kind of weirdos you might have dug up?'

'It's Mark's job to make every effort he can to contact relatives of our patients,' Meg argued. 'Gemma's mother was young, so her parents, possibly her grandparents, are likely to be alive. It seemed to us that they might have lived in the country or interstate, but had missed the earlier appeals for help in identifying her. They could have been on holidays, or overseas on business when the police flashed their messages across the country.'

She didn't add that she had paid for the photograph and a short message to be placed in every daily and weekly paper in Australia. To her, it seemed unbelievable that no one would recognise the child, and, knowing Gemma, she was certain some loving family, somewhere, would want her returned to them.

'It was a risky thing to do,' the woman persisted, 'but I suppose, as nobody responded, it hasn't caused any harm.'

Meg bit back her exclamation of surprise. Surely the department would be as anxious to find some relative of Gemma's as she and Mark—not to mention the entire hospital staff—were?

'Anyway,' the woman continued, 'I've come to arrange for her to go to a foster family we use in situations like this. It's only a temporary placement but it's the best we can do at the moment.'

She's not a situation! Meg wanted to yell, but she couldn't afford to offend the officious visitor.

'She'll need one-to-one attention from whoever is caring for her, and frequent visits back to the hospital for physiotherapy,' she explained. 'If the muscles in her thigh start wasting she will have trouble adapting to an artificial limb.'

The visitor frowned, and Mark, seeing her consternation, heaped more problems on her.

'And she's booked to go to Brisbane next week, isn't she, Dr Groves? And weekly visits after that for fittings and rehabilitation?'

'Our foster mums are excellent,' the visitor assured them, 'but they're busy people, and have other children to consider. We believe a family environment is the most appropriate place for children, but it's impossible for one child to be singled out to receive the bulk of attention.'

'Don't you have someone who could take Gemma on her own? Surely a family is still a family with only one child?' Meg asked, seeking a more acceptable compromise but contrarily hoping that the woman's response would be negative. 'She's suffered so much already, she needs extra-personal attention for her psychological as well as her physical well-being. She needs someone with the time to fuss over her a little.'

She drew a deep breath, and watched the woman's frown deepen. Was this the moment to spring her next suggestion?

She glanced at Mark, who nodded his approval.

'We could keep her here a little longer,' she said carefully. 'Quite a few of the staff already visit her regularly, and take her out on their days off. We could work a roster to take her to physio and eventually to Brisbane for the fittings and rehabilitation.'

'It would give you more time to find someone who might be willing to foster her with a view to adoption later, so she could go straight from here to a permanent home,' Mark added quickly.

He was strengthening her argument, Meg knew, but her heart jolted erratically in her chest when he mentioned adoption.

'She's been in the hospital far too long already,' the woman said crossly. 'We social workers also study psychology, you know. This is not the place for her.'

And a temporary foster family with a hoard of noisy, mobile, two-legged kids is? Meg wondered. Gemma's confidence, her self-esteem, was so fragile that she'd been shifted from the children's ward within days of her arrival in hospital.

The noise and good-natured teasing, the sight of other children being visited by parents, had distressed her so much that she had slipped into a dark and lonely world of her own, refusing food or attention, crying noiselessly all day and lying sleepless through the nights.

'Well, you've two weeks or so to decide.' Mark's voice, at its most placating, interrupted Meg's thoughts. 'The specialists have to run those tests to make certain the staphylococcal infection hasn't spread higher up the leg. Didn't you say they would take a fortnight, Doctor?'

He was ushering the visitor back out through the door, and Meg hoped her surprised mumble sounded like assent. So far she and Mark, with the support of other hospital staff, had contrived to keep Gemma out of official hands through strictly ethical processes. With one blatant lie, Mark had stepped beyond those bounds, and her agreement put her right beside him.

'At least worrying about you has taken my mind off the other bombshell that fell on my head today,' she told the sleeping child as she sank back down into the chair, shivering her reaction to the tumultuous events of the day.

An image of Jonathon rose up in her mind, and she squeezed her eyes tightly shut, trying to blot it out. Could she put her fingers in her ears to deafen the sound of his voice?

Think of Gemma! her instinct for self-preservation urged, and she opened her eyes and looked again at the child.

She had been lying as immobile as this—unconsciously still—when Meg had first seen her, one ankle swathed in the bandages the A and E department had used to stop the bleeding from the mangled joint. The X-rays from the two young men who had been injured in the same accident had come through first, and she had gone up to Theatre and started work, piecing together the shattered bones that were the usual outcome of car crashes.

Meg watched Gemma sleep, remembering how she had fought to prevent the police questioning the desperately ill child; how, right from the beginning, she had appointed herself as Gemma's protector. She was no more than a baby, maybe four years old at the most. And that first night she had looked so frail and white, and broken, that Meg's heart had gone out to her.

Then Mr Staines had been admitted. She blinked her surprise. She hadn't connected the two occurrences until this moment, but Gemma had been the child awaiting her attention when she'd first examined Mr Staines' wrist.

The realisation brought her thoughts full circle. Why had Jonathon ignored her as she had left the courtroom at lunchtime? Hadn't the relationship they had shared warranted at least a nod? Some compassion when he questioned her? Some sign that she had once meant something to him?

But she could have nodded herself, or acknowledged his presence in some way, she argued silently.

He was the one who left! her mind shouted. Surely it was up to him to make that first move?

Meg slid a hand across Gemma's soft hair, but this evening the child's presence failed to provide the solace she needed. The churning uneasiness in her body, the jumbled bits of past and present jostling for attention in her mind, had her so unsettled that she feared her emotional state might transfer itself to the tiny patient.

With a sigh of regret—for so many things—she rose to her feet, looked down once more, then turned and walked noiselessly out of the room.

'I thought I might find you here,' Bill greeted her when she emerged into the wide corridor. 'I cut the cast, and found some redness and swelling round the ankle.'

'And?' Meg prompted.

'And I tested for compartment syndrome. There is no additional pain from the flexing or extending of his toes but I checked the compartment pressure to be certain. No problem there, but he did confess he's been trying to lose weight and taking some unprescribed diuretics on a fairly regular basis. Because they're not prescription drugs he didn't mention them when he was admitted, and his GP didn't know about them, so no one told us.'

'So his body, left on its own to rid itself of fluid, has slowed down, and it's a fluid problem rather than a surgical one,' Meg finished. 'I wish we could convince patients to tell us *all* the things they put into their mouths.'

She was looking directly into Bill's grey eyes as she spoke, and caught the look of surprise. Had he been expecting her to blame him for not knowing about the patent medicine? Was she usually so quick to judge?

Yes, you are—where work's concerned! a voice responded in her head. Not her voice, but Jonathon's. It had been another bone of contention between them, another subject once debated but finally argued with the destructive passions of anger and bitterness.

'Have you put him on a diuretic?' she asked, struggling to maintain a rational flow of conversation while her stable world was tilting on its axis.

'I have, and cut the soft sleeve beneath the plaster and replaced it with a loose bandage. Then I wrapped the plaster back around the limb with elastic bandages. Do you want to check?'

He looked appealingly at her, like a large, friendly dog anxious for his master's praise.

'I don't need to check, Bill, you know what had to be done, but, if you're still here in an hour, see him again before you leave. Easing the constricting cast should have relieved all the pain by then.' She paused for a moment, then added, 'You'll find you'll sleep easier if you know you've guessed right.'

And with a final smile—thus creating a record for one afternoon, her cynical shadow told her—she turned and walked away.

Had Jonathon's attack so shocked her that she felt a sudden need to be liked? Was that why her usual detachment, her cool aloofness, had slipped so drastically?

It was dark when she left the hospital, and too cold

for the light summer suit she'd put on this morning to
wear to court. Navy linen might look businesslike, but
it provided little warmth on an early autumnal evening.
She rubbed her hands up and down her arms, thought
for a moment about taking a cab home, then shook
her head and set off at a brisk walk towards her flat.

Her mind swung between the past and present,
between the emotional upheaval Jonathon's totally
unexpected reappearance had caused and the dilemma
of what was to become of Gemma.

She tried to concentrate on Gemma, to convince
herself that before long a kind couple would be found
to adopt the little girl, to love and cherish her as much
as she deserved. But, even when she could bring herself
to believe that such people did exist, it didn't soothe
her. Deep within her heart she knew *she* wanted
Gemma, wanted to adopt the little girl and bring her
up as her own.

And that was impossible! She had a career that
demanded one hundred per-cent attention, and goals
she had not yet achieved. Getting on to the orthopaedic
programme had been the first step along the way.
Qualifying at the top of her year had helped get her
the hospital job, but it had only been another stepping stone. She wanted it all! First, head of surgery at
Shorehaven, then further specialisation, maybe microsurgery!

Objectively, she knew she did not have the time to
give to any child at the moment, let alone one who
needed so much of it for the next few years, to rebuild
not only her mobility, but also her trust and security
and love.

She also knew how difficult it was for a single woman
to adopt a child, and how much red tape and restric-

tions she would have to negotiate if she decided to take that path. So, even if all the other parts of the dilemma could be solved—which they couldn't be unless she gave up work—it would still be a battle.

And could she give up her work?

That was always the final stumbling block—the big brick wall that blocked off further unprofitable speculation. The very idea was so horrific that her mind ceased working at that point, and she hastened to assure herself that government departments usually knew what they were doing, and something wonderful would eventually turn up for Gemma.

As ever, these soothing thoughts failed to convince her, and she mooched along the street towards her flat, head down, and new leather shoes scuffling on the pavement as uncharacteristic depression flooded through her body.

'I was beginning to wonder if I'd have to sit on these cold, hard letter boxes all night!'

Jonathon's deep voice came out of the dark shadows by the front gate. The light edge to the words could denote teasing, but he had also used it to hide emotion. She couldn't guess at his emotions but the cadence was so familiar that it hurt.

'If you wanted to speak to me you could have done it at the courthouse at lunchtime, rather than skulking here in the bushes,' Meg pointed out as fear and anger catapulted the pain from her body.

'I don't think the judge would have liked to see the defence barrister hobnobbing with the prosecution's witness—especially before I'd had a chance to cross-examine you. You must have worked that out, Meg; you're not stupid.'

Now he sounded defensive, she realised. She stood

stock-still in the darkness and shivered from head to toe. Was he less assured than he made out? Were the words he needed not flowing so easily off his glib tongue?

'And is speaking to me more acceptable now, here in the dark where no one can see you?'

'Oh, for heaven's sake, Meg! I wanted to talk to you. I couldn't earlier, but I had your address. I tried to phone you, but you weren't in, so I decided to come here and wait for you.'

There was a long, tense pause that screwed Meg's nerves tighter and tighter, but she couldn't think of a single word to say—and doubted her ability to speak, if, by some chance, the words had been available.

'I hadn't counted on the darkness, although I should have known you'd head straight back to your precious work the moment you left the court.'

She tested the words against her memories, and heard the shading that was his impatience with her professional attitude. Nothing changed!

'I rather hoped you might invite me in. That we might be able to meet again as friends.'

His voice was more placating now, but Jonathon had always been able to use his voice to great advantage, whether distracting her from an argument, or seducing her to greater abandon during their lovemaking. She had realised long ago that he would make a good barrister, because of that one special gift.

'So, do we go inside?'

She peered into the darkness, sensing a movement, then he stepped forward into the splash of light thrown from an upstairs window. Even in the gloom his face looked grim, as if he was clinging to the last remnants of self-control, but she couldn't answer, couldn't force words out through her dry, numb lips.

She dipped her head, and stepped onto the path in front of him, leading the way towards the far corner of the complex, where her neat, two-bedroomed flat was tucked away behind overgrown shrubs and leafy bushes.

CHAPTER THREE

UNLOCKING the door, Meg pushed her way inside, reaching automatically for the light switch. Jonathon was one pace behind her. Every nerve cell in her body shouted his nearness, yet she couldn't slide away—or turn around and face him in the blaze of light.

He had stolen her ability to move, to think, to act.

Until he touched her! She felt his hands settle on her shoulders and spun away from him, colliding with the solid leather armchair she had found only last week in a country antique store.

'Why should we be friends?' she snapped, bending to rub a bruised ankle.

'Why shouldn't we?' he asked, stepping forward and reaching out a hand to help her balance herself.

His touch pierced her skin with red-hot needles of desire, and shame at her reaction brought a wave of heat to her cheeks. She shook the hand away.

'Because I'm not as sophisticated, or civilised, or worldly as you!' she informed him angrily. 'And I see no reason for us to pretend to be something we're not!'

She straightened as she spoke, and caught a momentary darkening of a shadow in the green eyes that looked so intently into hers.

'We were friends before we were lovers, Meg.' A deepening of his voice brought shivers up her spine, but she knew it was a trick of the trade—something he practised for use in court.

'Not for long,' she countered, battling to retain some

control over a body weakened by his presence, and a heart that had skittered into overdrive when he had dropped the word 'lovers'. 'And, anyway, why does it matter? So you've come back to Australia, but it's a big place. We're not likely to be running into each other every day of the week.'

His lips tightened and she wondered why her words had angered him.

'We ran into each other today,' he said stiffly, 'in circumstances that made it impossible for me to talk to you. I thought it was only polite to seek you out and apologise.' There was a strained pause before he added, 'For some unfathomable reason, I imagined I was glad to see you and, in an even more unlikely thought process, I wondered if you might be pleased to see me.'

Of course I'm not! she wanted to yell, but the lie stuck in her throat. She closed her parted lips and breathed deeply, trying to repel the waves of awareness arcing across the space between them.

I can't still feel like this about him, she told herself. It's shock, or tiredness, or hunger—

'Have you had anything to eat? Would you like some dinner?' She blurted out the words before she had time to think of the consequences, and there he was, nodding and half smiling, as if he was pleased about something. Totally distracted now, she turned away, fleeing to the kitchen as if it might offer a sanctuary from her thoughts.

She peered into the refrigerator and groaned. She had intended shopping after she had finished in court, but shock had driven such mundane considerations from her mind. Closer examination revealed a half-empty bottle of milk, a tub of butter and two apples.

She crossed to the cupboard, although she knew it would offer little more inspiration.

After the refrigerator, it looked overstocked with its two packets of breakfast cereal, a loaf of sliced bread, jar of honey and six tins of salmon. A packet of teabags completed the assortment, the lid open but the bags neatly aligned.

'Salmon on toast do?' she called, then realised he'd followed her into the kitchen, and was staring into her bare cupboard.

'At least when I lived with you I made certain you ate properly,' he growled. 'It's no wonder you're so thin, if your dinner every night consists of salmon on toast.' Then he stepped back, shutting the cupboard door, and turning towards her with a warm smile. 'Come on, I'll take you out to dinner,' he coaxed, 'for old times' sake.'

For a moment she was tempted, but the thought of sitting across from him in the dim lights of a restaurant sent her pulse-rate rocketing, and she shook her head, desperately seeking a way to hide her volatile reactions.

Maybe putting up with his company for a while—having a 'talk'—in the security of her own home was a good idea. If she acted as if his presence wasn't fazing her in the slightest then he would go away and not bother her again. She could cope with her own internal problems later!

'For old times' sake, I'll make you salmon on toast,' she announced calmly. 'It's still my most successful culinary accomplishment.'

'Salmon on toast it is, then!' He propped himself against the bench and folded his arms.

'You could go and sit down in the other room,' she

muttered, unnerved by his presence in the small room.

'I might be able to help,' he argued. 'Once upon a time I cooked all our meals.'

'"Once upon a time" is fairy-story stuff,' she snapped, pushing bread into the toaster, then rummaging through her cutlery drawer in search of an elusive can-opener.

'We were fairy-story stuff once.'

His voice was seductively soft, licentiously low. It quivered along her nerves, and danced in her brain.

'We were closer to fable, Jonathon,' she replied, stabbing the can-opener into the tin and releasing the pungent smell of fish. 'A warning to others of how not to become involved. Whatever good we had built up in our relationship we unravelled through our disagreements.'

She glanced up, waiting for an argument that did not come. Instead, he shrugged, and reached across to lift the toast out and drop more bread in place.

'Do you believe that?' he asked when the task was completed.

'Of course I do! We were heading off in totally different directions. Couldn't talk things through any more, couldn't seem to find a middle ground where we could both meet.'

There was a long pause, filled with the soft scraping of the knife as she buttered the toast.

'Even our lovemaking was affected by it,' she added sadly as memories of those violent consummations flashed like film re-runs through her mind. Right from the beginning of their love-affair, the intensity of her emotions had terrified her, making her feel totally out of control. But towards the end the passion that anger had fuelled to fever pitch had been like a desperate, driving need that nothing could assuage.

'I rather thought the arguments were a symptom, not the disease,' he offered, and she looked sharply at him. He had moved away from the bench and was peering out into the darkened garden, and suddenly, more than anything, she wanted to feast her eyes on the lean, well-sculpted face, with its neat dark eyebrows, long, thin nose and mobile lips.

She needed to stamp this image in her mind, to update her mental pictures so this new, more mature Jonathon could take their place.

'A disease?' she asked when the continued silence strained the air to a brittle tension.

'Or maybe a disability.' He turned back to her now, and shrugged. 'The problem was we had different priorities, wanted different things. The timing was all wrong.'

'When we first met, we had shared dreams, Jonathon,' she said, slapping salmon on the toast and squashing it down with the knife. 'Could you pass the other pieces of toast?'

His fingers slid across hers as he handed her the warm, fragrant slices.

'Did we, Meg?' he asked softly, green eyes gleaming down at her. 'Apart from the intention of spending as much time as possible in bed together, did we have any other mutual goals?'

'You were halfway through a medical degree when you arrived in Australia. We had our studies, we talked about practising together,' she reminded him.

'Did *we* talk about it, or did you? You knew I had studied law for three years first, and switched to medicine because I wanted to go deeper into ethical issues, medical ethics in particular. Shall I carry this through to the table?'

She nodded, pleased to have him out of the kitchen, but puzzling now over this new contention. She finished her 'cooking' and followed him to the table, watching as he lifted a piece of toast and bit into it with strong white teeth.

'Well?' His gaze did not waver from her face, and the tone of the words dared her to deny what he said.

Her chin tilted. She wasn't one to refuse a dare!

'But you loved medicine!' she pointed out. 'You were brilliant at it. When we decided to live together, when we made that original commitment to each other, I thought you'd be happy to make that your life. I thought we'd make a good team, a partnership in all aspects of our life.'

'In orthopaedics?' he teased. 'If you had known me at all you should have realised that, of all the medical specialties, it would have had the least appeal to me. It suited you, Meg. It fitted your innate sense of tidiness, your love of neatness. Bones were controllable. They had nice, clean lines, and, even broken, they could be put tidily back together. It wasn't like oncology, where cancers might rampage willy-nilly through the body, or gynaecology, where babies might not arrive on the due date.'

She heard the words, and wondered if they held some seed of truth—oversimplified, of course, but essentially true? Perhaps, but *her* personal ambition hadn't been the only issue.

'When you decided to switch back to law, I supported you,' she objected, although his decision, at the end of a medical degree with only one year's work in a hospital to complete his qualifications, had been incomprehensible to her at the time.

He reached out and covered her hand with his.

'I know you did, Meg, and worked like a slave to keep me while I studied, but it was a singular ambition—my dream, not ours.'

'Well, people must have their own dreams!' she muttered, disconcerted by the feelings his hand was reawakening, and unable to understand where he was heading with his words.

'But people making any form of commitment to each other should have some they share as well! That's what I'm trying to say. That's what we didn't have. For heaven's sake, we couldn't even agree about the form of that commitment.'

Meg shook her head. He had wanted them to get married—right from the start—but she had held out against legalising their relationship. Her own experience, as the eldest of seven children, had made her suspect marriage was a trap—for the woman. She had seen the subtle shifting sands in marriages, seen the wife's priorities changing from career to housewifery, and it had frightened her.

At her insistence, they had made their own private vows on a mountain top—and broken every one of them in time! Sadness vied with the heat that was sweeping over her in a consuming wave. Then Jonathon was speaking again and she had to drag her mind out of the past.

'At times it seemed as if we had nothing in common,' he murmured.

'Apart from bed!' she reminded him, peering down at the cold toast as if it might explain the excitement stirring back to vibrant life within her. But Jonathon had always had this effect on her—calling up a strident sexual hunger simply by walking into the same room. It blotted out reason, and clouded all other issues, so anything seemed possible, as long as they were together.

The hand that covered hers tensed, his fingers sliding into her palm, digging into its sensitised centre—sending silent messages she found harder and harder to ignore.

'Apart from bed,' he echoed. 'But, as you said, our disagreeing over just about everything else was destroying the one beautiful thing we did share—our lovemaking, our passion.' His voice deepened as he spoke, the rich timbre of it sending shivers of delight down Meg's spine.

'So why did you insist on this meeting?' she asked, angry that her body was betraying her mind. She slid her hand away from his, and clasped it to its mate on her lap. 'If we weren't able to sort things out four years ago, why should we try now? Maybe if you'd stayed—'

'I couldn't stay,' he said, so definitely that he startled her, and the flames of desire faded to a fitful glimmer.

'And I couldn't go,' she said quietly, sadness sinking into her heart.

'I'd worked so hard to get to where I was. The position I was offered on the orthopaedic programme couldn't be deferred, you knew that! It was a once-in-a-lifetime opportunity.'

'The clash of the mighty careers! Dreams that led in different directions!' His words were as full of shadows as the eyes that watched her from across the table.

'We were young,' she argued, saying the words her mind had said so often. 'We had plenty of time before we had to decide about marriage and children. We had the rest of our lives to go tripping off around the world. But no! Once you'd decided you wanted to go back to England, it had to be right then, and it had to be a honeymoon!' Her voice rose, and she pushed her chair back and breathed deeply, trying to relax the knots twisted inside her.

'I shouldn't have forced you to make that choice.' It was half-statement, half-question, but she was unable to reply, for beneath the words was a sadness that echoed in her soul.

'Well, it probably turned out for the best,' she said. 'You've obviously found a career you enjoy and are good at—' she squashed the bitter taunt she would have liked to add. Something in his voice had told her this was the time for placating, not arguing '—and I'm so busy with work that I barely have time for a life outside it.'

'So you're happy?' he asked, and this time she uttered the lie.

'Very!' She said it defiantly, mentally tossing her head, but her hands gripped each other beneath the table, her nails digging into the palms as she willed herself to remain outwardly calm and unconcerned.

'All the time, Meggie?' he whispered, and the words seemed to slide across her skin in a physical caress. 'Even at night when heat burns through you and you remember how it used to be? Even then, have you no regrets? Even then, don't you wonder whether a career with a capital C is worth any sacrifice?'

He was making love to her with his voice, although his tone was still confrontational. Unable to resist him, she felt a shuddering release throughout her body as years of pent-up tension began to melt away. If only they could make love, everything would be all right.

Yet, as the seditious thought slid to the surface of her mind, she denied it. Leaping back into bed with Jonathon was not going to solve anything. And after the way he had treated her in court! She hadn't finished with that issue yet.

She shook her head slowly, and picked up a piece of toast, although it would do nothing to satisfy the deeper hunger.

Why had he come back if all he wanted to do was go over their old arguments? She ate another finger of toast. Maybe she should ask him. Maybe it was her turn to contribute to this conversation.

The phone saved her, jangling into the silence so loudly that it startled her. She glanced across at Jonathon, and knew from the deprecating grin exactly what he was thinking. So many of their 'discussions' had been cut short by the phone—by a summons to rush back to the hospital for one reason or another.

'It doesn't happen as often these days,' she said quickly. 'That's more likely to be Mum or one of the family.'

She saw his eyebrows fly upwards, and the smile turned rueful. As an only child, brought up by a widower father, he'd been unable to comprehend her attachment to her large, unruly family, or accept their dependence on her.

'Well, whoever it is, hadn't you better answer it?' he teased, smiling at her obvious reluctance.

Meg eyed the instrument cautiously. It had to be the hospital! Anyone else would have decided she wasn't at home and hung up by now.

She forced herself to stand up, to move—to reach out to silence the noise.

'It's Gemma, Dr Groves,' a quavery voice that could
have been any of the ward night nurses told her. 'She's
gone right back to how she was when she was first
shifted up to our ward. She's lying stiffly in the bed
with tears rolling down her cheeks. She won't talk to
any of us, or tell us what's wrong—nothing!'

Meg felt the blood drain out of her body. She
remembered the afternoon's visitor. Had Gemma been
awake after all? Had she been feigning sleep and heard
something of that conversation?

'I'll be right up,' she told the caller, and dropped
the receiver back onto its cradle.

Jonathon was watching her, a slightly sad but still
sardonic smile twisting his lips.

'Duty calls, huh?'

And suddenly Meg didn't want to go. Suddenly she
knew how he must have felt all those times she had
simply walked out of their 'together life' and back into
the world from which he had excluded himself.

'It's a child, Jonathon. I amputated her leg a few
weeks back. She's been extremely ill. She's got no
family, no one.'

The realisation that she was cold returned, and she
rubbed her hands ineffectually up and down her arms,
wanting him to say he understood, that he wasn't
angry, that he would come back some other time and
talk to her.

'How did you end up with a child who has no
relations?' he asked. 'Were her family all killed in the
accident?'

So much for his being angry! His quick mind had
seized the diversion and zeroed in on the problem.

'Her mother had hitched a lift with two young men,
who knew Gemma's name and nothing else. They were

both injured, but Gemma's mother was killed. Police enquiries throughout Australia and New Zealand haven't produced a single relative.' She spoke flatly, repeating words she had said so many times.

He whistled softly, obviously intrigued by the legal aspects of the untraceable child. 'That's a curly one! And what's the problem now? Complications with the amputation?' he asked. 'Is she having phantom pains? Or trouble with a neuroma forming?'

Meg shook her head, wishing it were that simple, although either problem would cause concern.

'It's more psychological than anything. In the beginning, when we were trying to save the damaged leg, we nearly lost her several times because she had so little will to live. She can't remember or tell us anything. She is so alone.' She watched his face, hoping to see it soften into understanding. He frowned as he absorbed the words, and her heart gave a painful twitch. That little pucker of his eyebrows while he was thinking! She had forgotten that.

'Why did you have to amputate in the end? Did the long bones not mend?' he asked, and she realised he had been dredging back through his medical knowledge. She met his enquiring green gaze and answered honestly.

'The tibia and fibula weren't the problem, but the ankle was crushed and I had to pin that. There was always a chance it would have to be re-pinned as she grew, but I was confident that she would walk normally. . .'

'And?'

'She picked up a staph infection,' she admitted slowly. 'All hospitals are having problems these days, no matter what new sterilisation and disinfection techniques they adopt. It's been present at Shorehaven, but well under control and whether it was Gemma's age, or her general debility. . .'

Again her voice faded away. The thought that Gemma's leg might have been saved if she had been in another hospital was one that haunted her day and night.

'And is all the staff concern over the child a manifestation of collective guilt?'

Jonathon's mocking question speared through her, and the shock must have registered on her face, for his smile slid away and a full-blown frown of annoyance appeared in its place.

'Go and get something warm to put on,' he said crossly, dismissing her pain. 'Do you drive now, or were you walking home because you still refuse to become part of the twentieth century and buy a car?'

'It's not far to the hospital.' She skated around the issue, ashamed to admit how fearful she was about learning to drive. Heading for her bedroom to find a warm jacket, she added, 'And walking is good, healthy exercise!'

Not waiting for his reply, she continued on into the little bathroom, and splashed warm water across her face. She was too thin and too pale to look attractive at the moment, and her dark eyes seemed grotesquely large in her tired, drawn face.

'I'd have liked to look nice for Jonathon,' she whispered to her reflection, then she shook aside the futile thoughts and hurried out. It didn't matter what she looked like—there was far too much animosity in both of them for peace to ever be proclaimed!

He had washed the two plates and put them neatly away, and was waiting for her by the door.

'I'll drive you,' he announced, taking Meg's elbow and ushering her out of the flat, 'and wait to drive you back. You shouldn't be walking the streets on your own after dark. Did the infection get into the bone and spread up the leg? Was that why you had to amputate?'

He guided her towards a dark shape by the kerb and helped her in. She sat stiffly in the leather seat, watching his easy movements as he walked around the bonnet and climbed in the other side.

'Yes, but now it's not the infection or the wound,' she repeated, trying to keep her voice level and free of the emotion that was churning her insides to mush. 'Her leg is healing beautifully, but there are psychological scars we can't mend as easily. She's been so cheerful and positive lately—a normal, happy, healthy little girl. But tonight. . . The nurse who rang seems to think she has sunk back into the old depression—'

'And where do you fit in, Meg?' he asked, so quietly that she knew it was only a preliminary question. She waited for the follow-up. 'Don't tell me you're doing a surrogate-mother thing?'

The derision in his voice cut through her like a burning sword. She had denied him a child once; had refused to break her career-building for the time it would have taken to produce a baby for him. 'Come back to England with me, have a baby, take some time off!' he'd begged, but she'd known one baby could lead to another. He hadn't understood how trapped it had made her feel, how threatening such a future had seemed.

Tears spun across her vision, and clogged her throat. She hadn't wanted marriage and certainly hadn't wanted children, not back then when she had been learning through experience every minute of each long

day—when she'd been offered the position she had
wanted so badly! She'd had so many dreams for herself,
and children weren't part of them—not then.

They pulled up outside the hospital.

'Thanks for the lift,' she mumbled, not wanting to
be parted from him, yet knowing there was no point
in their being together. Some wounds went too deep
for words to heal. 'I'm sorry about being called away
like this, but perhaps it's for the best. I don't think
we can be friends.'

'I said I'll wait for you,' he repeated, ignoring her
final remark. 'And I will wait, Meg.'

She shrugged and shut the door, her mind so confused that she couldn't think straight. Worrying about
Gemma usually took precedence over everything, but
tonight the thought of seeing Jonathon again later both
excited and terrified her. Had her relationship with
the little girl softened her, and made her vulnerable?

Jonathon watched her race into the building as if
pursued by demons. Well, there were enough demons
sitting on his shoulders these days; surely Meg had
some as well. She was upset about the child—he'd
sensed that.

The thought had no sooner firmed in his mind than
he was out of the car. He had gone to see her to find
out if they could meet as friends. Shouldn't a friend
be more supportive than simply sitting in the car outside? He hurried through the doors, but she was gone.

'I'm looking for Dr Groves,' he told the smiling
woman on duty behind the reception desk. 'She came
in to see a child.'

'Little Gemma,' the woman said, nodding as if everyone should know which child Meg would be visiting.
'Fourth floor, turn right when you come out of the

lift, and she's in the third room on your right.'

He nodded his thanks and headed for the lifts, uncertain now about what he was doing. He found it hard to believe that Meg was taking a personal interest in a child—Meg, who fretted and worried over her younger siblings, yet had refused to bear his child.

Anger bubbled up within him, a curdled, frustrated rage that was as unexpected as it was unpleasant. The lift doors opened and he looked into the wide conveyance, half tempted to take it up to the fourth floor so he could strangle her, and half tempted to walk back to the car and drive away. It had been an insane idea from the start, this wanting to see her and 'sort things out'.

He had imagined Meg in many situations. When he was feeling confident and cheerful he always saw her sad—pining for him. In his more depressed moods, she invariably had a lover, and he would drive himself back to work, losing himself in complicated cases until he forgot everything but the present moment. But for her to be caught up with a child—that was the unimaginable!

And if she was personally involved, did he want to witness that involvement?

The compulsion that had been the driving force throughout their relationship pushed him into the lift and he followed the receptionist's directions, no longer attempting to answer the unanswerable. The desire to see another facet of Meg was overwhelming.

The murmur of her voice came through the half-closed door, and he paused, unwilling to intrude at what might be an inopportune time, although the still angry part of him wanted to burst in and denounce her as a hypocrite.

'I won't let you go to anyone unless you're happy about it, Gemma,' she was promising. 'Do you think all your friends here, people like Kim and Margie and Mark and Bill, would let anyone take you away unless you wanted to go?'

Had some family member come forward to claim the child? Jonathon wondered. If that was the case, they had a right to take her. The anger faded as the legal issues flitted through his head. Surely Meg couldn't be making false promises to her patient? Jonathon pondered, wishing he had asked more about the child's circumstances.

'We've got another two weeks to work things out, sweetheart.' He had to strain to hear the words—she must be bending closer, whispering them.

Did he have a time limit on his quest to work things out, to settle things between them so he could get on with his life? Would he have two weeks—or two minutes—if she found him hovering here and was upset by his presumption? That was the trouble with Meg—one could never be one hundred per cent certain! Trouble with him as well, he admitted, if he looked at himself honestly. Did he really want to work things out?

He heard movement in the room, and another quiet whisper. He stepped away from the door and leaned back against the wall, trying to look nonchalant and unconcerned. But her face when she emerged destroyed his composure, for tears were sliding down her thin white cheeks, and her teeth were sunk into her bottom lip as if to stop herself from crying aloud.

'Come on, Meggie, I'll take you home,' he said, sliding an arm around her shoulders and drawing her

close against his chest. He walked swiftly to the lifts,
half hiding her, knowing how much she would hate
other staff members to see her distress.

CHAPTER FOUR

MEG woke with a sense of unease that deepened when she remembered that Jonathon was sleeping in her spare bedroom. He had hurried her out of the hospital, then bundled her into his car, stopping on the way back to her flat to buy a bottle of wine.

'Good for shock,' he'd said as he had insisted she drink a glass. 'You've had a few too many of them today.'

His eyes had gleamed with a teasing laughter, and her body had responded with a ferocity that had frightened her, but she'd pushed herself back into the big leather chair and pretended she drank wine with ex-lovers every day of the week.

They'd talked about Gemma and the legal ramifications of an unidentifiable child—safe conversational ground because it didn't carry haunting echoes from their shared past.

Then she'd agreed to let him stay—because he'd had a drink and hadn't wanted to drive—and she'd said goodnight and fled to her bedroom, to lie awake for most of the night, longing for the feel of him beside her, and the release that only his special magic could achieve.

She raised her hand to her face and tried to brush away the memories. It was eight o'clock! Her watch face, turned upward with the movement of her arm, showed she must finally have fallen into a sound sleep—and overslept. Not only overslept, but was still in bed well past the time she usually left for work!

She pushed aside the covers, and dashed into the bathroom, showering quickly. As she emerged, towel-clad and damp, the cause of her sleeplessness appeared outside the second-bedroom door, his wide chest and broad shoulders bare above bright boxer shorts, his skin so pale and satin-smooth that her fingers tingled with a need to touch it. She gripped her towel more tightly round her body, and scurried to her bedroom to find clothes that might mask her confusion.

Dressing hurriedly, she assured herself she wasn't running away from Jonathon, or the situation, but that she always left for work this early—earlier, in fact!

Fully clothed, she bent over the dressing-table and smoothed cream clumsily into her pinker-than-normal cheeks, then swiped some lipstick across her lips. She was ready!

Crossing the room, she tapped on the bathroom door. 'I'm sorry, but I have to go. Please help yourself to tea or coffee, and there's cereal and bread for toast.' He knows that, she reminded herself, but she had to say something. 'Just pull the door closed behind you when you leave—it locks itself.'

She half caught his reply, the words muffled by running water, muted by the door. Had he said something about seeing her later, or was it hope that had twisted the words to sound like that? Nothing had been resolved between them, but was there any need for resolution? They had met again—and survived the meeting. Why should they expect more?

'Late night, Doctor?' her anaesthetist teased when Meg pushed her way into the staff changing-room. She knew Brian didn't for one moment believe that social

pleasures might have been the cause of her tardy
arrival. It was well known that she could work till two
or three in the morning, and yet be the first of the
theatre team ready for action on an operating day.

She opened her mouth to use Gemma as an excuse,
then closed it again.

'Very late night,' she agreed, and turned away to
don her theatre garb, ignoring the open-mouthed
astonishment of her colleague.

She forced her mind to switch over to work, to concentrate on the operating list for the day.

'Mrs Atkins is an asthmatic. Have you spoken to
her about the anaesthetic?' she asked Brian.

'I saw her earlier,' he assured her. 'I've explained
I'm going to use a muscle relaxant and mild anaesthesia. Her attacks are usually controlled by Ventolin,
so I'm not anticipating any major problems. It's the
next patient, the man with the bunions, who worries
me. Normally we'd do a spinal, but I think I should
use a general anaesthetic for him as well. He's a nervy
type and has a history of unstable angina. I wish we
could go back to the old days when patients came in
the night before an operation, and anaesthetists had
more time to consult with the patients.'

Life's back to normal! Meg thought. Brian com-
plaining about the way the hospital rushed through
their surgical procedures was a regular Thursday-
morning lament.

'I think the patients prefer to come in on the day
of their operation,' she told him, 'although it does
make it awkward for you fellows. Perhaps you should
start consultations in rooms; then we could send our
patients on to you after we've booked them in for
surgery. Would that be better than seeing them for

the first time three minutes before you send them off to sleep?'

'Don't joke about it,' he grumbled. 'It's hard enough to do this job when you feel as if you're guessing half the time, without you well-paid aristocrats of medicine mocking us!'

Meg grinned at him, and they walked through from the scrub-room together. He was an excellent anaesthetist, and she enjoyed working with him, although the detached professionalism that had made him choose a specialty with little patient contact irritated many of the other surgeons at the hospital.

Bill appeared and slipped the ultrasound films of Mrs Atkins' left knee into the viewing screen. An arthroscope two weeks ago had revealed that the medial meniscus, one of two crescent-shaped disks of cartilage that helped the knee move smoothly, was damaged beyond any hope of repair. A meniscectomy, or removal of the damaged meniscus, was the only solution, as the torn cartilage would continue to become irritated and inflamed if it remained in place.

Originally Mrs Atkins had been Bill's patient, Meg remembered, sent to him by a mutual friend who played A-grade tennis with the injured woman. Perhaps now was the time to give her back to him!

'It's far too physical an operation for a woman to do,' she told Bill as they approached the operating table.

He looked at her in stunned silence, his eyes wide and shocked above the pale green mask.

'One of my professors told me that when he was trying to dissuade me from studying orthopaedics,' she explained, chuckling at his surprise. 'Today it's my excuse to let you operate.'

She saw shock, and a trace of fear, flash through

his eyes, then excitement banished everything else. Was she throwing him in at the deep end? No, she decided. Knowing he was assisting in the operation, he would have studied the procedure last night—he was the most conscientious student she had ever known. And he'd assisted her at three similar procedures and knew how she worked.

'I'll have the end of the table removed,' he told the theatre orderly, his voice crisp with new-found confidence, 'and sit to do it.'

Meg nodded behind his back. She always sat at the end of the truncated table, with the patient's foot in her lap. It gave her more control over the joint, and she could manoeuvre the knee more freely to get at the tricky posterior horn of the ligament. It *was* a strenuous operation for a female surgeon, although she wouldn't have admitted that in anything but a joking fashion.

'Will you wrap the leg?' Bill asked, and she moved quickly into the less familiar position of assistant.

A nurse slapped a flat rubber bandage into her hand and she began to wrap tightly, from toes to thigh, to reduce the blood supply to the leg. Bill slipped the tourniquet around the thigh and she watched as he tightened it, restricting the blood flow even further.

He moved efficiently, and Meg found she was watching as if this were the first operation she had ever seen. He cut through the skin, then through the fibrous capsule that surrounded the inner edges of the joint. Once through the membranous layer, he bent and extended the joint until he had the optimum visibility through the narrow opening.

'Hold this,' he said briskly, and Meg took the retractor, while he slipped a hook around the nearer horn of the meniscus and cut it free from its attachments.

Now that there was one free end, he could grasp it more tightly, and she saw the toothed forceps slipped into his waiting hand. That had been the easy part. Getting a clean cut at the other end was far more difficult because of other uninjured ligaments nearby that had to be protected.

She found herself holding her breath, willing him to succeed—suddenly more involved on a personal basis than she had felt for a long time. She smiled delightedly into her mask as Bill manipulated the cartilage over the top of a curved scalpel and cut it cleanly away.

'Well done!' she said. 'But don't think you can hand over to your assistant for closing. I want you to do the lot.'

Bill checked the wound carefully, seeking any final fragments of the damaged meniscus that he might have missed, then neatly sewed up the three layers.

'I'll bandage it,' he said, turning to her with his delight shining in his eyes. 'Should I put a cast on as a temporary splint?'

Meg shook her head. 'She's a sensible woman and I've told her she'll be confined to bed for the first two days. After that you want her moving it, to maintain muscle tone in the quadriceps. Send the physiotherapist to see her tomorrow. She'll work out a series of exercises for her.'

With the restricting bandage and tourniquet removed, they turned away from the patient, leaving her with the anaesthetist and post-operative staff who would wheel her away.

'Thanks, Meg!' Bill said as they stripped off their outer layers in the scrub-room.

'Don't thank me,' Meg responded, grinning at his

obvious delight. 'You'll be doing more and more of my work as the year progresses. I should be thanking you. How's Mr Rogers?'

'He's comfortable this morning,' Bill assured her, 'and the swelling round his ankle has disappeared. Would you suggest a new solid plaster cast before we send him home?'

'We'll think about it. He'll have to be weight-bearing and using crutches competently before we can think of discharging him. He lives alone and will need to be able to care for himself. Once he's on his feet, we'll have a better idea of how the plaster will stand up to the stress.'

They were gowning up again as they talked, and Meg had turned so Bill could tie her tags when the nurse poked her head around the door.

'Next patient's in, and the third one—the other knee—has been cancelled. His GP rang this morning to say the man's got the flu and won't be able to come.'

'I wonder if there's anyone on the public list we could contact in time to get them here and prepped?' Meg mused, tugging at her gown to get it comfortable. Her mind did a rapid scan of patients who were waiting for elective surgery.

'I wouldn't look for more work,' the nurse warned. 'There's a pile of messages waiting for you outside, and one of them is something about going back to court.'

Breath whooshed from Meg's lungs, and she reached out and grasped the edge of the sink for support.

'I thought the case was over,' Bill said. 'Or your part of it, at least.'

'So did I,' she muttered, battling to regain her composure. She thought back furiously, scrabbling through disjointed memories of the previous evening. At no

time had they mentioned the court case—not after her
initial outburst, anyway. She hadn't asked if it was
over, and Jonathon hadn't volunteered any information. She had simply assumed, especially after what
he had said about the impropriety of the defence coun-
sel talking to a prosecution witness, that the matter
had been finalised!

Had he stayed with her because it was convenient?
And if the judge would frown on his talking to her in
the lunch-hour, how would he class staying overnight
with the witness?

'You OK? Did it rattle you more than you thought?'
Bill asked, peering anxiously at her.

'I thought it was finished,' she said with a shrug,
pretending an indifference she was far from feeling. 'I
can't think what else they'd want to ask me. Maybe
Maree made a mistake about the message.'

Her heart leapt at the thought. Maybe it was a message from Jonathon, but had come through from the
courthouse. That was it! she assured herself, and followed Bill through into the theatre to deal with Mr
Williams' bunions. But did she want a message from
Jonathon? Was there any point in seeing him again?

'The bunions are mine,' Bill was telling the
assembled staff. 'Dr Groves is assisting.'

She had 'given' him the bunions weeks ago, and
now, shaken as she was by the possibilities in one small
note on a table outside the door, she was glad she had.

In a worry-induced haze, she watched him open the
skin above the deformed toe, and carefully pull the
top tendon aside so he could remove the base of the
phalanx bone. She heard the murmured conversation,
and the buzz of the saw, watched the nurse swab the
site, removing any debris. Next he would cut away the

bony deformity on the inside of the metatarsal bone.

Her professional self watched the process, silently applauding his sureness, but the newly disturbed emotional self trembled with uncertainty, ready to retreat far back into its shell any moment.

'All done and we've earned an early mark, I think!' Bill announced at last. 'How about I shout us a late lunch in the canteen?'

She was pleased he hadn't suggested leaving the hospital, and hoped it was because he wanted to see the two patients later in the day. Post-operative patients were checked by the anaesthetist until they went back to their rooms, and then became the responsibility of the doctor on duty in the wards. All specialists called daily to see their hospitalised patients, but Meg believed that this daily call should begin on the day of the operation. She liked to see her patients after an operation, although often they were too sleepy to talk to her, and too drugged to be feeling any pain.

'Sounds good,' she told him, 'but I'd better check my messages first.'

Surely the case was over? Let Maree have been wrong. She tried to divert her mind, to think of something else.

'And I'll have to call in and see Gemma on the way down. She was upset last night—terrified about being sent somewhere strange to live.'

Bill turned towards her, his eyes full of understanding and sympathy. 'Wherever she goes, it will be strange at first, Meg,' he said softly, but she shook her head, denying the truth she could not face.

'I'll see you down there,' she told him and hurried out of the room so that the conversation couldn't continue.

Four of the five messages concerned patients, but the fifth sent a flood of ice through her veins.

'Contact Chris Wells at the courthouse', it said, in the hurried block letters of her secretary. A phone number followed the message, and Meg stared at it in horror.

'We need you down here as soon as you can make it,' Chris told her on the telephone minutes later. 'Peter has already been granted an adjournment until we could contact you. He can ask for it to be extended if you can't get here this afternoon, but the judge might not grant it. We go back into court in fifteen minutes.'

'I'll be there,' Meg told him. It was easier to go along with him than try to think with brains that had turned into scrambled eggs.

As she emerged from the staff-room, Bill appeared.

'I've got to go back to court—now,' she told him. 'Could you please call in and see Gemma for me? Tell her I'll visit her as soon as I finish at court.'

Bill patted her shoulder reassuringly, and she realised how frazzled she must be looking for him to take such a liberty.

'I'll take her down to the canteen with me. She can have afternoon tea while I have lunch.'

Meg glanced at her watch. Three o'clock already! How long ago had the judge granted the adjournment? And what would have happened if she had been in Theatre with the patient who hadn't turned up?

'Thanks, Bill,' she said, and hurried towards the lifts, wondering what they would have done if she had said she wasn't available. Would it have mattered? Could she have done that, within the law, or was she obliged to go?

At least her mind had returned to some kind of working order, she realised, hurrying along the footpath as if her life depended on her getting back to the place.

For what?

The question slowed her feet and accelerated her heartbeats. So that Jonathon could put her down again? Could make her appear ineffective?

But he wouldn't do that, her heart argued. Not now, not today, when they'd parted as 'friends'!

Chris was waiting at the bottom of the shallow steps leading into the building. He seized her arm and hustled her inside.

'Peter's stalling at the moment,' he said, pulling her into the waiting lift. 'He said to apologise for dragging you back, but he wants the jury to hear your "maiming" evidence again. He's anxious you try to use that actual word. The other fellow blathering on after you'd given your evidence would have confused the jury, or left what you said less clear in their minds.'

'But that could happen again,' Meg protested. 'Once Peter puts me back on the stand, the other fellow—' forget he's Jonathon, she warned herself '—can do exactly what he did last time.'

Chris shrugged. 'Well, he could,' Chris admitted, 'but it's closer to the end of the case and there's more chance of the jury remembering what you said when they go off to make their decision.'

They were at the door of Court Four, and Meg found that her knees were trembling. Her heart jostled about in her chest at the thought of seeing Jonathon, although common sense told her he could not acknowledge their 'friendship', and instinct warned it would be a far from pleasant encounter.

'Wait here till they call you,' Chris instructed, and Meg sank gratefully into a chair. Now she remembered she'd had no breakfast, and lunch was something she had only talked about with Bill. Perhaps if she fainted from hunger they would excuse her! she thought, then realised that she often worked through longer days than this without food—or fainting.

'Come in, please, Dr Groves.' It was the same young policewoman.

Meg smiled at her, then followed her into the court.

'You are still under oath, Doctor,' the judge informed her as she stepped up into the witness box. 'And, presumably, the prosecution needs you to clarify something. I trust they are not wasting either your valuable time or mine!'

The steely disapproval in his voice made her wonder what had happened in the case, and she wished she had asked Chris how it was going.

Peter was on his feet and walking towards her, and she kept her gaze fixed on him. She was afraid to look at Jonathon, afraid of how her body might react if he did not nod or smile or acknowledge her presence in some way. It didn't matter how much she told herself he couldn't do that in this court-room; her wayward senses were not ready to believe it.

Peter apologised for interrupting her day, for having to bring her back down here. He made it sound as if it was the defence's fault that he had been forced to recall her.

'. . .especially as I have only one question to ask you,' he said, and she tried to gather her disordered thoughts together and concentrate on what was happening.

Peter looked from her to the jury. Was he reminding

her to direct her answer that way? She checked the twelve, wondering how the delay had affected them. The overweight man looked thoroughly bored and one of the women had a distracted expression on her face, as if she was worrying about who was minding her children, or what she would cook for her husband's dinner.

'If Mr Staines' wound had not been treated immediately,' Peter asked, dragging her attention back to him, 'what would have been the outcome?'

She'd forgotten the word Chris had told her to use! Deformed? Contracted?

'Without surgery to repair the tendon, the hand would have contracted and ended up bent forward like this.' Again she demonstrated with her hand, but now warning bells were flashing through her mind. Peter had said 'immediately', and she had performed the surgery that night—because it was easier to repair the tendon before it retracted too far. Easier but not impossible.

Would Jonathon remember that from his basic medical training? He was standing up, bending over the table, shuffling through his papers. He would be coming towards her any minute!

No, she assured her panicky heart. It was during her specialty training she had studied surgery of the forearm and hand. General surgical procedures in fifth year would have covered some of it, but not in sufficient detail for him to contradict her.

'Dr Groves.' The words, and his nod, were an acknowledgement of her presence, nothing more, but she could not halt the riotous leap of her senses, or the searing rush of heat through her body. His gaze flicked across her face, then he turned his profile to her so he could watch the jury as he spoke. 'You say that contracture of the hand would result if surgery was not used to repair the tendon?'

'That's correct,' she quavered, trying to appear as composed as he was.

'Immediately?' he asked, and her heart stopped beating. It doesn't matter! These people—Peter, Chris, Mr Staines—mean nothing to you! You're an expert witness and all you can do is tell the truth. Her mind screamed the assurances at her, but she knew, deep down, it did matter.

'As soon as possible,' she said firmly, silently admitting that if he persisted the point would be lost. She felt failure squeeze the life from the irrational excitement of seeing him again.

'And how immediately is "as soon as possible"?' he asked in dulcet tones, turning to her with gleeful anticipation glinting in his eyes. He was as sure of victory as she was of failure, she realised, and a sickening wave of defeat swept over her.

It doesn't matter, she told herself again, but repetition didn't make it easier to believe.

'The longer the tendon is left unrepaired, the more difficult it is to fix satisfactorily.'

She directed the words at the jury, then glared at Jonathon, who had the temerity to wink at her. It was a game to him, she realised, but the thought failed to cheer her. She remembered long hours of Monopoly, when he would refuse to concede defeat, playing on and on until luck turned his way. Even in play he loved to win, and court-room battles must be considered the greatest games of all!

'And how long after an injury would you confidently say you could repair a tendon? How long could Mr

Staines have waited before it became too bad for a competent surgeon like yourself to repair?'

It was a trap—she knew that—but she couldn't remember the exact details pertaining to the legal parameters of unlawful wounding and grievous bodily harm. Was it that an unattended injury would cause permanent damage, or an injury not treated immediately? Whichever it was, she had to answer the question Jonathon had asked.

'I can't say,' she objected, stalling for time while she tried to think, 'because deterioration depends on many other factors. But you have to remember that the tendon wasn't the only injury. If Mr Staines hadn't sought medical help he might have bled to death, and, as you said yesterday, what does a maimed hand matter to a dead man?'

He nodded as if to grant her a point, then bored straight in again. 'Wouldn't wrapping the wrist tightly have stopped the bleeding?'

'It might have,' she told the jury, 'but that is supposition because he did come to hospital, and the artery was repaired at the same time as the tendon.'

'But supposing he hadn't?' the wretched man persisted, hammering away at his point until she felt like hitting him. 'How long after the tendon was cut would it have become too retracted to repair?'

'Three to four weeks.' She flung the words at him, incensed that he would treat her like this, although she knew her anger towards him, personally, was unfair. He was doing his job—and doing it well.

'So "immediately" is now "three to four weeks"?' he repeated softly, but it wasn't a question and she certainly wasn't going to respond. He wasn't right, she knew that! He had twisted her words into a meaningless jumble and Peter's ploy of bringing her back to the stand had failed.

Then Jonathon was gone, and Peter was on his feet again, asking her the same question he had asked earlier. The jury shuffled in their seats, tired of the professional antics and bored silly by the semantics.

Beside Jonathon, Peter appeared an amateur. Had he been as easily defeated in other aspects of the case?

She was thanked for her co-operation and asked to step down, and she hurried from the court, carrying an illogical burden of defeat with her.

It doesn't matter, she kept repeating to herself as she walked back towards the hospital. We need never see each other again, in spite of Jonathon's weird concept that they meet as 'friends'.

Maybe there wouldn't be other occasions. She shook her head. The reason he had studied medicine was because he was interested in the development of medical litigation—a whole new sphere of law as patients began to see their medical advisers not as the gods of old, but as ordinary fallible human beings. And could they ever be 'friends' if the bulk of his work involved fighting her professional colleagues?

The random thoughts chased each other through her mind but her body denied her rationality. Surely it couldn't be harbouring hopes of a reconciliation? There was more to a relationship than sex, she reminded her wayward heart.

Her feet flew along the pavement as she fled the unanswerable questions. She tried to think of Gemma, and the problems that were escalating in that direction, but images of Jonathon flashed across her mind, blurring her thought processes.

'I went down with Bill for lunch,' Gemma told her

happily when she walked into the small, brightly decorated room.

'That's great!' Meg responded, bending to kiss the flushed cheek. 'On crutches or in the wheelchair?'

'I went on crutches,' the little girl announced. 'Bill said he'd catch me if I fell. He'd make a lovely father, wouldn't he?'

The innocent question teased at Meg's heart. Gemma needed a mother *and* a father. She deserved the best in every way!

It was the clincher that always brought her own dreams to an abrupt end. And if she did juggle her work, if she could cut through the red tape and adopt the child, Gemma would still be fatherless!

Somehow she responded to Gemma's question, and talked and laughed with her, but her mind darted off on its own track.

Would the few dates she'd had with Dave Waring, the ophthalmologist attached to the hospital, lead to anything?

The thought died a natural death. That first surging flood of hormonal activity in the court-room—that one wild swoop of internal elation when her body had recognised Jonathon—made a mockery of anything she felt for Dave.

'Do you like Bill?' Gemma's voice broke into her thoughts.

'He's great!' she replied, wondering if a four-year-old could read minds, or if Gemma's question had been purely coincidental.

She left Gemma when the physiotherapist arrived, promising to be back early in the morning, then went up to do a ward-round before going home. Janet Greene handed her the small yellow message slip, and even before she read it she knew what was written on it.

'I'll see you later!', it read. Unsigned as his notes had always been. Had it been an arrogant assumption that there could be no one else of great importance in her life? Was it still that?

She tried to feel anger at his presumption, but none came, blotted out by questions she shouldn't be asking. What time would the court case finish? Would they sit late, if it could be completed today? Did the barristers have to wait around for the jury to make their decision?

Again she wished she knew more about court procedure, and she was conscious of an urgency within her as she checked on her patients.

Because, she admitted reluctantly, in spite of the pain of the past, and what had happened in court today, she wasn't strong enough to resist the urge to see him—just one more time.

There was no strange car outside the flats, no note to say he had called stuck under the door. Should she be glad or sorry? Glad that she could shower and change, that she could try to look her best although she knew she shouldn't want to!

Then she saw the book. It was open on her desk as if whoever had been reading it had left hurriedly. Without moving a step closer she knew it was her book by Lampe, *Surgical Anatomy of the Hand*.

Had he left it open deliberately? Was it some subtle message?

Numb with shock, Meg hurled herself towards the bedroom, seized a suitcase and began ramming clothes into it. She had no faith in her treacherous body's ability to withstand Jonathon's excuses, and could not bear the thought of another argument which she would be certain to lose. Words were the ideal weapons for Jonathon, the tools of his trade.

Escape was the only solution, and, as a holiday town, Shorehaven had a multitude of hotels, motels and guest houses from which to choose a refuge. She left through the back door, taking a path from the rear of the building to the next street, then walked around the corner to the main road, where a passing taxi picked her up.

'Where to, lady?' the cab driver asked, and Meg's mind went blank. 'Running away, are you?' he joked while she tried to think of the name of one local hotel or motel.

'Somewhere near the hospital,' she stammered, then realised Jonathon would look there first—if he was going to bother to look. . .if he even became aware that she had fled! 'Not too near, but somewhere quiet within walking distance.'

Had she been stupid, running away like this? Perhaps the note was from someone else, and Jonathon had no intention of coming back to see her. He'd got what he had come for—the information about the surgery she had performed, she reminded herself bitterly as the cab swung through the lamplit streets.

But he could have found the same information in any medical library, hope argued.

'The Regal Motel—this do you?'

The vacancy sign was flashing, but, behind the gaudy neon colours, the motel looked welcoming. Light gleamed through well-trimmed shrubs, and tall palms threw patterned shadows across a low-set brick building.

'I'm sure it will,' Meg responded, but uncertainty shimmered like a haze across her thoughts. She climbed out of the cab and followed the driver, who was carrying her case towards the reception area. She was telling herself that she had overreacted, and contemplating asking the driver to take her back home, when her pager buzzed. She lifted it and read the message sliding across the small screen.

'I'm at your place, where are you?' it read. 'Ring me on. . .' There was a nine-digit number that told her it was a mobile phone, and this time the message gave a name—Jonathon!

She shoved the small black machine back into the bottom of her handbag.

'I'd like a room for a few nights—I'm not certain how many,' she told the receptionist, and paid the cab driver while the woman began her paperwork.

He hadn't lost any time, if he had her pager number already. Then she remembered that she had left in such a hurry that she hadn't switched off her answering machine. At the end of her polite 'I'll call you back' message she gave her pager number for use in emergencies only.

'Room fifteen, through the courtyard and over at the end. You'll find it quiet and peaceful, Dr Groves.'

Meg blinked, and looked more closely at the woman. She had given her name, but never gave her professional title.

'You did my husband's hip last year. Reg Edwards, remember?'

'Of course! I'm sorry I didn't recognise you, Mrs Edwards.' Meg completed her registration as hurriedly as she could. 'How is Mr Edwards?' she asked, signing her name at the bottom of the form.

It was a good question, as the friendly woman was able to give an up-to-date account of her husband's problem all the way across the courtyard.

'I hope you'll find it comfortable,' she finished. 'Are you shifting house that you need a place to stay?'

Meg's mind whirled. She hated any kind of prevarication, but Mrs Edwards' curiosity would be aroused if she didn't give a satisfactory reason for seeking refuge in a motel.

'P-painting!' she stuttered, remembering how she wished she had shifted out the one and only time her flat had been painted.

It was obviously acceptable, for, when Mrs Edwards finally left her alone at the door of the room, she was still reminiscing about the places she had lived in while painting had taken place around her.

Her pager buzzed again, but it was Jonathon repeating his message. She stared at the little black box and wondered again if she had overreacted. Then she remembered how eagerly she had hurried home, feet flying in response to the urging of her body and its quixotic desire to see him one more time.

Years ago they had pushed aside all rational arguments against their living together in the heat of what could only be called lust, and, for a while, their shared delight in each other's bodies had drawn a curtain over differences that had, in time, become irreconcilable.

To go back to Jonathon now, if only on a temporary basis, for the pleasure he could give her aching, frustrated body would be emotionally disastrous; no, worse than that, she told herself, flopping onto the wide double bed—catastrophic!

CHAPTER FIVE

THE buzzing of her pager came into a dream where her sisters and brothers, young again, were rampaging round her flat, scattering books in all directions while Jonathon sat in an armchair and frowned his disapproval.

It should have been a nightmare, but Meg woke smiling, then gazed around at the unfamiliar surroundings, taking a moment to work out where she was. Asleep, fully clothed, on a bed in a motel room—that was where she was!

Had she overreacted? The memory of those minutes in her flat made her shudder, but she knew that the past was repeating itself. Jonathon had always affected her natural ability to think things through; had destroyed her instinct to rationalise, rather than emotionalise, issues and decisions.

Surely he isn't calling again? she thought, reaching into her handbag to silence the machine's persistent noise. She pulled out the little black box and read the latest message.

'Please contact hospital urgently'. Words that had become familiar over the years scrolled across the screen. 'Tourist coach accident, all hands on deck'.

The end of the message jolted her. It might not have been strictly professional, but it was certainly to the point. She leapt off the bed, and hurried into the small bathroom, stripping off her clothes as she went.

You'll have to eat, she reminded herself as she

81

towelled her body dry and scrambled into clean under-
clothes. Call a cab? No! If she cut through the park,
the hospital was only five minutes' walk from here.
That would be quicker.

She reached for the phone and rang the hospital
switchboard to let them know she would be available
in fifteen minutes. That would give her ten minutes in
the canteen to feed some carbohydrates into her
system. There could be a long night in Theatre stretch-
ing ahead of her.

The counter staff at the canteen, who always seemed
to know everything that happened in the hospital
within seconds of its occurring, filled her in as she
selected and paid for her food. Egg sandwiches—
carbohydrates and protein!

'Coachload of Japanese tourists, coming back from
a day up the mountains. Seems part of the road was
weakened after all the rain we had last month. The
edge gave way, and sent the coach rolling over and
over down the slope.'

Meg cringed inwardly at the relish with which the
details were relayed, but she knew the innate kindness
of these volunteers who staffed the canteen twenty-four
hours a day. She made no comment, except to murmur,
'Sounds bad, doesn't it?' before paying for her meal
and walking away.

'Called you in as well, have they?' One of the theatre
nurses looked up as she walked towards her, and Meg
nodded and smiled, plonking her tray on the table and
dropping into a vacant chair.

The young woman was rosy from sleep, gulping at
a cup of coffee as if the caffeine in it would work some
instant magic. 'I swear this is the fifth time I have
spent a day working so hard that my feet won't hold

me up a moment longer, and they ring me within an
hour of my falling into bed. It never happens after
we've had a slack day!' she complained.

'That's fate, I guess. What about all the poor tourists
who were probably thinking of a hot shower, followed
by a huge steak and seafood dinner when their bus
plunged off the edge of a mountain?'

'I suppose it's slightly worse for them,' the girl con-
ceded with a smile. She drained the last dregs of her
coffee and pushed the cup aside. 'I might see you in
Theatre some time during the night,' she added before
hurrying away.

Meg bit into another sandwich and watched her go.
Was there a husband or a lover in the bed she'd left?
There were hundreds of people employed in the hospital, all with their separate 'outside' lives, like little
circles that never touched except within the one over-
lapping section that was their work.

'If Dr Groves is in the hospital, would she please
report to the fifth floor.'

The message came tinnily through the call system,
and she responded automatically, picking up the
remaining sandwich to eat in the lift. The fifth floor
housed the theatres, and she could imagine the buzz
of activity that was taking place there at the moment.

Bill was waiting for her in the corridor outside the
first theatre.

'I've a fractured femur in Theatre Three,' he told
her, 'a nasty open wound that I'm going to pin intern-
ally; Jack Weston is in Two, pinning a shoulder.
They're keeping all the simple fractures downstairs and
the residents and registrars on duty are handling those,
but there's an elderly woman with a posterior hip dislo-
cation come up to Five. There is also significant blood

loss from a gaping wound in her arm, so they're getting her ready for a full anaesthetic.'

'If someone is operating on her arm, I can't ask for her to be put in a prone position for a reduction. I'll have to use the Allis manoeuvre to get it back into place—and that means I need help from someone who knows what he's doing!' She half smiled at Bill, wanting him to want to help her. 'If she's elderly, I don't want to have to try twice. I could end up causing more damage than an open reduction would.'

Bill grinned. He's enjoying all this drama, Meg realised, then remembered that she had enjoyed it once herself. It was a special excitement, fed by adrenalin, when tired bodies forced themselves on and on, battling whatever challenges were thrown their way.

'What if we scrub and do the hip, then I'll go back to the femur? They'll have found something else for you by then.' He ushered her into their changing-room. 'I know there's a suspected broken hip in X-Ray, and still a line of people in A and E waiting for films. It seems the coach driver saw the depression in the road and slammed on his brakes, and the sudden jarring caused as many problems as the subsequent roll.'

'Who's downstairs deciding priorities?' Meg asked, pulling her theatre cap on and tying it firmly into place.

'Don Grayson was here visiting a patient. Seems he leapt into the fray with such enthusiasm that no one liked to ask him to leave.'

Meg smiled. Don Grayson was a senior consultant and one of the panel who had provided her own training. Nowadays he did little public hospital work, preferring to operate and visit his patients in one of the smaller private hospitals.

'Well, at least he knows what he's doing,' she said.

'It's better than some poor first-year resident trying to decide which patient we should see first, who needs surgery and who doesn't.'

They walked together into the theatre, greeted the staff already assembled there, and moved to the end of the operating table. The woman was as slight and frail-looking as a child, and Meg's heart lurched as she remembered her first glimpse of Gemma.

The X-rays were lit up and she studied them for a moment, then nodded and crossed to the table, running her hands around the exposed and badly distorted hip.

'We're all done at this end,' an unfamiliar voice told her, and she glanced at the woman who had spoken. She must be one of the new staff in General Surgery, Meg realised, nodding a greeting.

'I'll keep that husky-looking sister you've got there, and the rest can take a break,' she said, smiling hello at Brian, who was on the anaesthetist's stool. 'If you could put your hands here,' she told the male nurse she had asked to assist them, 'and hold her pelvis steady.' She demonstrated what she wanted. 'Bill will flex the knee, and apply longitudinal traction while he flexes the hip. With any luck, I'll then be able to rotate the joint back into its socket.'

As they moved into position she glanced again at the unconscious patient.

'Remember she's an elderly woman and her bones are likely to be fragile,' she warned the two men, 'although I don't know if the Japanese have as much trouble with osteoporosis as westerners do. Whatever happens, we don't need to add a broken pelvis or any other damage to her woes.'

They moved into position, and she held her breath, her hands working almost of their own accord as they performed an action practised until it had become second nature.

She heard a slight click, then Bill's sigh of relief, and smiled her delight at her helpers.

'She's all yours,' she told Brian, then picked up the patient's chart to complete the relevant details before she departed. 'I'll put her down for another X-ray as soon as she's well enough to be moved again,' she told Bill, 'in case she goes to the general-surgery ward not ours, and no one thinks of it down there.'

'I'll check up on where she goes later,' he replied, and Meg knew he would. He was going to be a great orthopod, she decided, and felt pleased she was involved in his training.

An orderly appeared with more X-rays, and Meg took them with her into the ante-room so the theatre could be cleared and readied for use again.

The film showed a fracture at the head of the femur. The accompanying information told her the patient was another Japanese, a male, aged seventy-one. He must have been conscious when examined, for his consent form was signed by him, not someone acting on his behalf. His bones showed up white as if the bone density was good. That would promote healing in spite of his age.

Meg looked at the break, which showed clearly as a black shadow across the bone. With bed rest and traction the bone could mend itself, but bed rest held other risks for elderly patients, and, as a stranger in this country, wouldn't he be anxious to get home as soon as possible, so he could recover among friends and family, in a hospital where people spoke his language?

If she pinned it, he could travel much sooner,

although the wound of the surgery for the open reduction would bring added pain and inconvenience.

Robyn, the theatre sister on duty, returned to say they were ready, and she told her what she planned.

'I'll need a sliding hip screw, a small size, maybe one we'd consider for an older child, and will fix the plate to the femur with the smallest-gauge screws we can use. He's a slight old gentleman, from the look of these pictures. Did they start him on a drip and anti- biotics downstairs?'

'Yes, and the lab's sending up matched blood now. The orderly who brought him up says there are at least another seven people who will need reductions, so it's only the beginning.'

'We should be thankful the ones we get are alive. Knowing that road, I'm surprised we've got patients to treat.'

'The coach driver is in Intensive Care—head injur- ies,' Robyn told her soberly, 'but he's the worst. I wish he could know he probably saved the lives of all these people.'

'Maybe he does,' Meg told her, surprised by this show of sympathy from the normally pragmatic Robyn.

They walked together back into the theatre, Meg moving towards the small area of visible skin, the only part of the patient, apart from his head, that was not shrouded by sheeting.

Do I like this job because it's neat and tidy? she wondered, as she made her first incision. Did I choose it because I can deal with generally fixable bits, and not have to worry about the whole person?

Jonathon's words haunted her as she worked, cau- terising tiny blood vessels, separating stringy muscle

fibre, until she reached the bone and could begin her
reconstruction work.

Carpentry, he had used to call it, she remembered
as she drilled into the bone to make an opening for
the sliding screw.

Her fingers flew, selecting the tools she needed, then
discarding them again, moving swiftly to minimise the
trauma to the patient, and lessen the chance of
infection.

Surely the hospital had finally beaten the staphylococcal bacterium that had haunted it for the last few
years! Methicillin-resistant staphylococcus aureus or
MRSA was becoming increasingly common, especially
in hospitals where so many antibiotics were routinely
used. There was a higher element of risk in orthopaedics, where pins or other foreign objects were
forced into the patient's bone, making an opening
through which bacteria could infiltrate.

'You nearly done?' Brian's voice interrupted her
thoughts.

'Is there a problem?' she asked, glancing worriedly
at the screen that monitored the patient's heartbeat
and breathing.

'No, but I didn't want to give him more than the
minimum amount of anaesthetic. The translators can't
cope with medical terms, so no one knows if any of
these patients have drug-related allergies. I'm giving a
balanced anaesthesia because it's fast-acting, and, by
using small amounts of a number of drugs, I'm hoping
to stave off any major side-effects from an excess of
any particular drug, but it's difficult to monitor the
degree and duration, so I'd like you lot to be in and
out as soon as possible.'

'Two minutes,' she assured him, beginning to close

while Robyn flushed the wound, and her assistant passed her sutures. Brian's warning remained in her mind, and she thought about the problem he was facing with each new patient.

'Perhaps I should go downstairs and see who is listed to come up,' she said to him as he prepared the patient to be transported to Post-Op. 'With many of the fractures, we might be able to use traction to keep them stable and delay the operations until we can get someone with Japanese and medical knowledge to help translate.'

'I think you'll find there are plenty of patients who will have their operations delayed without any intervention from you,' he said drily. 'I walked through A and E when I got here. It was like a bomb-site. There were forty-three people on that coach, and I doubt there's one that won't require hospitalisation.'

'So what's the priority if we do get a medical translator? How many people know if they are allergic to particular drugs, let alone anaesthesia?'

Brian smiled. 'True!' he admitted. 'Which is why we poor anaesthetists live on hope. Right now I hope you're going to get me a cup of coffee and something sustaining to eat and have it ready when I get back from Post-Op. I've got a second-year resident holding the fort for me in there. Says he wants to specialise in anaesthetics, so this should either convince him or cure him of the foolish idea!'

Brian departed and Meg let a nurse help her strip off her gloves, then peeled off her gown and dropped it into the big garbage bag. She checked the theatre, watching as another nurse carried a tray of instruments through to the autoclave.

Business as usual, she thought, and realised that she

hadn't thought of Jonathon for three hours.

Well, she'd thought about what he'd said to her, about his caustic comments on her career choice, but not about him as a person—not with the pulse-accelerating, heart-stopping, wild elation of the senses that had accompanied her home earlier in the day.

And, thankfully, she had no time to think about him now, either. She'd promised Brian coffee, and needed something to drink and a handful of biscuits herself.

They worked on, meeting for snatched reports in the theatre ante-rooms, or during brief rests in the staff lounge between shifts at the operating table. Meg felt the tiredness creeping up her legs, and turned to look at the big wall clock. Five-thirty! It had been a long night, but she knew that this was the last. This patient must have caught his hand between seats, and had mangled it badly. She and Bill were both working over it, she using sutures crimped into microscopic needles, to bring together severed arteries and nerves, while Bill aligned the bones and pinned them into place.

As she stitched a severed tendon back together she remembered the court case, and wondered how it had ended. She should have waited to see Jonathon, she thought, and faced up to him. She should have found the words to explain her feelings of betrayal—not run away!

But it was easy to think that way here, safe in the heart of the hospital, in the theatre where she was the expert. Would she be as brave outside these familiar walls? And did she want to face up to him?

He had hurt her so badly, going back to England with a stubborn, contrary insistence that had defied explanation. She didn't want to risk that pain again, she told herself firmly. Jonathon was part of the past and it was no good trying to turn back the clock.

'Did you win that argument?' Bill asked, interrupting thoughts that had flown too far away for sense.

She looked up at him, and saw a glistening spark of humour in his eyes.

'Weren't you arguing with yourself,' he teased, 'frowning so ferociously and muttering away into the poor chap's wound?'

'Maybe I was,' Meg admitted, shaken that even thinking about Jonathon could distract her so completely.

'Whatever it is, there's not much you can do about it in your condition,' Bill told her as he stitched lacerated skin back into place across the palm of the patient's hand. 'We're off duty after this one. To try to do any more would be asking for trouble. Do you want a lift home?'

Now her flight to the motel seemed ridiculous! But did she want a lift home?

'No, thanks, Bill. I'll find a bed over in the quarters and sleep there for a few hours. Don't think the panic's over because we've survived a hectic night in Theatre. The wards will be bulging by now, and all the staff called on last night will have to be replaced for today's shifts. Chaos will reign supreme!'

'Not so as anyone would notice,' Bill said, handing the suture needle to his nurse. 'To the visiting public, it will look like any other day. Hospitals only seethe beneath the surface—like some people I know.'

He shot a questioning look at her, and she wondered if she'd been muttering aloud when her thoughts had strayed to Jonathon.

'You're right, I was seething,' she admitted. 'It was

that court case. The defence barrister made me look foolish.'

'They do it all the time,' Bill said easily. 'It is their job, when all's said and done. Funny job, I'll admit, but they probably think we're a bit odd, considering our fascination with people's bones.'

Meg nodded, but stripped off her theatre garb more hurriedly than usual. She was feeling too fragile for philosophy.

'I'm going up to see Gemma, and will put my head into the ward and see that all's quiet, then go over to the residents' quarters for a few hours. You take the day off and I'll phone if we need you. Post-operative care for all these extra patients who are not used to our food, and can't speak our language, is going to be trying enough without both of us tackling it in zombie-ish states.'

'Will do, boss!' Bill said, snapping a salute at her.

Barriers were certainly breaking down, she thought drily as she hurried towards the lifts. She and Bill were veering towards the 'friendly' stage—a new occurrence in her life. Until recently, her fellow workers at Shorehaven had been colleagues, and, nursing wounds that had taken too long to heal, she had been happy to keep it that way.

The ward was as quiet and as calm as it could be with seven extra beds packed into it, and staff changing shifts. Meg saw the strain on the faces of the nurses going off duty. They had probably had a worse night than the theatre staff—having to deal with hurt, frightened, confused, conscious patients, not anonymous hips or hands.

She went from bed to bed, stopping at each and reading the new notations on the charts. Most of the new patients were sleeping, but Mr Rogers and the other 'old' patients were familiar with the routine. They had finished their early cups of tea and were now sitting up in bed wanting to talk about the accident.

She lingered with them for a while, then crossed the corridor to check on the Japanese patients who had been put into the smaller rooms. Only one problem at this stage, she decided, frowning over an elderly Japanese woman's temperature. It was the patient whose hip she had manipulated.

The surgeon who had stitched her arm had ordered intravenous antibiotics, but fever was definitely present. Could it be a drug reaction? She checked the drug again and made a note of its name and strength, then left to look it up. If a high temperature was an occasional or possible side-effect, she would feel relieved.

Half an hour later she was no wiser, although something was niggling at the back of her mind. In the same way that some conditions were more common in racially distinct groups of people, could drugs have different side-effects on Asian people from those they had on people of European origin?

Picking up the phone, she rang Administration. Mark Reynolds answered his cheerful voice full of enthusiasm although he, too, had probably been up all night.

'I might have known you'd be the one called in to sort this out,' Meg said, glad to hear his voice. 'Have you found a Japanese doctor?'

'One Japanese-speaking Australian chemist so far. He's coming in at nine. Do you think I should keep trying for the real thing?' Mark asked teasingly.

'Unless this fellow has lived and worked in Japan,

I think you should.' She explained her concern. 'So speaking to them and understanding what the patients are saying might not be enough, because few people would be aware of their reactions. Try the university. If they haven't a Japanese doctor on staff, they certainly have a big-enough Japanese population to know if there is one in this south-east corner of the state. If there is, I think we need him here urgently.'

She returned to the room where the worrying patient lay, and found the hospital's senior physician leaning over the bed.

'Trouble, Meg!' he confirmed wearily, and she realised that he had also been up all night. A nurse was applying cool compresses, while the young resident adjusted the drip.

Meg nodded. 'Her temperature's far too high for it to be anything normal with the amount of antibiotics she's received. I was wondering about a racial reaction to some drugs. Mark's trying to track down a Japanese doctor.'

The older man looked perceptibly brighter. 'Like PKU being more prevalent in people from the Mediterranean countries. I hadn't thought of that, but, now you mention it, I wonder if I have heard of race-related drug reactions.' He paused for a moment, and Meg imagined she could hear him thinking. 'No!' he said at last. 'Nothing I can recall. Let's hope Mark finds someone soon. I've stopped the antibiotics she was on and was about to try something else, but maybe we'll wait an hour or so and see what happens.'

'Do you want me to check on her again, then?' Meg asked, and was relieved to see him shake his head.

'No, you scuttle off home and get some sleep. We'll all be needed back on deck later today.'

Meg scuttled—but only as far as Gemma's room. She had to see her before she left, as who knew what might happen later?

'I thought you'd end up here at some stage.'

'Jon'thon's showing me how to make animal shadows!'

The deep voice and the fluting childish delight intermingled. The room was darker than normal, the main light having been turned off and the bedside lamp turned so it threw a spot of yellow on one wall.

A dark butterfly cut across the brightness, and Meg heard Gemma's gleeful chortle coming from a great distance as reality retreated.

'It's eight o'clock in the morning. What are you doing here?' she demanded.

'Showing me shadows.'

'Waiting for you.'

Again a chorused reply that made no sense at all.

'I know you've been up all night, but that coach accident didn't happen until two hours after I called at your place. You ran away from me, Meg!'

His voice was hard, demanding an explanation without putting the demand into words. He's angry, Meg realised as her own anger returned. And what right did he have to be upset? I'm the one who was used as a convenience then belittled in front of all those people!

Jonathon's fingers continued to move, and a rabbit now hopped across the wall. Gemma clapped then tried to twist her own tiny fingers into the right shape. Meg watched as Jonathon's large hands reached out and gently pushed them into place.

Gemma's mine! she wanted to shout. She recognised the burning wrath inside her as jealousy and felt sick that she could feel that way—could contemplate denying the child some extra pleasure—however fleeting it might be.

She walked across to the bed and reached out to touch the smooth cheek. Ignoring Jonathon, she spoke to Gemma.

'I've been up all night. I'm going to have a sleep now, but I'll call in and see you later, OK?'

Gemma looked up and nodded, secure again in her special world.

'I'll drive you home,' Jonathon said, turning the lamp so Gemma's fingers could reach in front of it and throw shadows on the door. 'And you, young lady,' he said, patting her silvery head, 'you can practise the animals I've taught you—cat and dog and butterfly and rabbit—and when I come back I'll show you some more.'

'I'm not going home,' Meg muttered, holding back the 'and even if I were you wouldn't be coming with me' that she would have liked to add! 'I have to come back in later, so I'll grab a few hours' sleep in the residents' quarters.'

With a final wave to Gemma, she stalked out through the door, but he was behind her before escape was possible.

'You shouldn't be in the hospital at this time of the day,' she said crossly. 'And as for walking into Gemma's room without so much as a by-your-leave—'

'I told her I was a friend of yours, and visiting because you were very busy and might be late coming to visit.'

He was striding down the corridor, following her, but so close to her right shoulder that her body could feel the heat of his all down one side.

'You had no right,' she repeated, 'and it's lax security on the part of the hospital to let you in. Patients, especially young ones, are totally vulnerable. That's why visitors are vetted by staff, and the staff in that ward had no right to allow you in there.'

They reached the lifts and she pressed the button then swung around to face him as she finished speaking, and found him far too close for comfort. He was smiling at her, that teasing lift of his lips that drew deep lines down his cheeks, but his eyes were wary, and she had to wonder what game he was playing now.

'Well, before you tear strips off the poor overworked staff for letting an outsider into your domain, perhaps I should explain that I told them I was your husband.'

She was so tired that she was imagining things, Meg decided, but the mocking glint in his eyes told her otherwise.

'You couldn't have!' she gabbled as the lift doors, tired of waiting for passengers to enter, slid silently closed.

'Why not, Meg?' he asked, the glint blinked away, replaced by hardness. He stepped away from her and pressed the button so that the doors opened again. 'It's not that far from the truth,' he added, ushering her into the void with a firm arm around her waist. 'Didn't we both agree that our relationship would be as meaningful as a marriage, that our vows were not to be taken more lightly simply because we didn't have a stranger with official status listening to them?'

The doors closed, leaving them alone in the shiny capsule. Suddenly the enormity of what he had done struck her, and rage at his deception threatened to swamp her.

'How dare you pass yourself off as my husband, then

justify it by talking of the promises we made to each other? What about those promises? Didn't we include consideration for each other, and respect, and caring? You come tripping back into my life—when it suits you. Then you barge into my place, and stay the night, for the sole purpose of reading up on hand surgery to use the knowledge against me!'

She spat the words angrily at him, too tired to care about the consequences any more. 'You used my own book to make me look stupid and ineffective! Why should I want to talk to you? I've heard enough of your clever talk to last me a lifetime.'

He let her finish, then reached out and held her shoulders.

'What happened in court wasn't personal, Meg. You're intelligent enough to know that! You must also know I hadn't intended staying the night, and that I could get that book in any decent library.' He shook her gently as the lift jerked and stopped. 'You're using your anger about the case as a shield, something to stop you thinking about the real issues between us.'

The doors opened and people flooded in but his hands held her clamped to the floor.

'There are no issues between us,' she said coldly, ignoring the startled looks of their fellow passengers. She shrugged off his hands and marched out into the foyer.

'Oh, no?' Jonathon demanded, grabbing her and turning her in one easy motion. 'Then what about this?' he asked loudly. He stepped towards her, bent his head and kissed her on the lips, his mouth demanding, seeking, teasing, punishing.

Meg felt her body sway slightly, and willed it to remain upright, to not seek his with the wanton abandon that thrummed through her veins. She told her lips to remain cold, and closed, to not respond in any way. His tongue teased at her skin, electrifying her nerve-endings, then, just as she knew she must give in, his head lifted, his hands dropped from her shoulders, and he turned his back on her and walked away.

CHAPTER SIX

MEG must have slept, for her watch said midday, but as she looked around the bare little room provided for staff on call she could have sworn she had barely closed her eyes.

Gemma, inexplicable fever and Jonathon all jostled for attention in her mind. Jonathon and his unfinished business! Could an attraction like theirs ever be considered finished?

She shuddered and turned her thoughts to Gemma, but sleep had provided no solution there either. She could not be kept in hospital much longer, she could not be adopted while a search was continuing for relatives, yet the temporary foster family idea was repugnant to Meg.

Sighing, she wrapped a skimpy hospital towel around herself and dashed across the passageway to the shower. Maybe clean, hot water would slough away her worries! Maybe Mark had found a Japanese doctor!

As she dressed, her subconscious pursued the one problem that rational thought might be able to solve. The sleep must have helped, she decided with a rueful smile at her reflection in the dusty mirror. Most of the patients operated on during the night would have received the same antibiotic, so if it was a racially related drug fever they should all be showing signs of the toxicity.

Relief flowed through her, but not for long. She might have been too tired to work that out earlier this

morning, but she hadn't been so tired that she had
missed Jonathon's strange confession. He had gone in
to see Gemma. Even now, she couldn't picture the
two to them together without a distinctly unsettled
feeling. And he'd called himself her husband! That was
a nice bit of gossip for the orthopaedic department to
chew over.

Perhaps they were too busy for it to be passed on.
She left the little room. The ward was her world and,
if it was seething with speculation, then it was better
faced sooner rather than later.

'Glad you're here,' Janet greeted her, with what
appeared to be a sidelong look.

You're imagining things, Meg told herself, but then
Janet was speaking again—and not asking questions
about a supposed marriage!

'I've a Japanese doctor creating chaos in my ward.
Mark tells me you insisted he find one, so it's up to
you to handle him.'

Seizing Meg's arm, Janet dragged her through to the
main ward, where beds were still packed more closely
than Meg had ever seen them.

A slim bespectacled Japanese man in an elegantly
tailored suit was issuing instructions to one of the
nurses. The young girl looked as if she was about to
burst into tears, and it was obvious that she couldn't
understand one word of what he was telling her.

Meg listened carefully. The stranger was definitely
speaking English, but, with his accent and the com-
plexity of the medical terms, it was hard to realise that.

She walked towards him, hand outheld, and introduced herself. His smile was one of utter relief.

'I am Sasaki-san. I cannot make the nurses understand that I'm not a doctor who can practise here. I am

a lecturer at the university, in microbiology, although I trained first to be a doctor,' he told her. 'They want me to do things I cannot do, I think—or maybe I don't understand either!' He held out his arms in a universal gesture of despair.

Meg smiled. 'Well,' she started slowly, 'as your English is one hundred per cent better than my Japanese, we will speak in English. First, I would like you to accompany me around the patients. I will explain what we have done for each of them, what drugs they are on and why, and how long we expect their recovery period to be. If you could tell them whatever a doctor in Japan would tell his patients in the same circumstances it would be a tremendous help. We will start with Mrs Shagisi, because I am worried about her temperature.'

The man nodded, and Meg turned to the nurse and asked her to find a drugs reference guide, so Dr Sasaki could check on the pharmacology of the drugs prescribed to each patient.

Meg led him to the private room where the elderly patient slept, her bright colour indicating that the fever had not subsided. She picked up the chart, glanced quickly at it, and passed it to the visitor.

'Because of the possibility of allergic reaction to penicillin, we used cephalosporins against post-operative infection,' she explained, pointing to the drug then looking into his face to see if he understood. 'This is the only patient who has shown a reaction, if the temperature is a reaction. I would have expected a rash, or some other manifestation if it was a drug allergy, but. . .'

Meg shrugged, and led the visitor forward, introducing him to the woman who had stirred when she had begun speaking, and was now watching them with bright eyes.

The doctor bowed, then spoke rapidly, and Meg was relieved to see her patient smile, and respond in a voice that sounded strong and positive.

Mrs Shagisi giggled shyly and waved one hand towards Meg.

'She does not know of any allergy and she has been given penicillin before without any adverse reaction. She says the other translator told her a lady doctor fixed her hip. She asks if that was you,' the doctor said.

'It was,' Meg said, smiling and nodding at the woman. 'But the arm wound was far more serious. One of our other surgeons took care of that.'

Dr Sasaki translated in an incomprehensible flow of words, and Meg watched the woman look at her bandaged arm in surprise, then speak again.

'She says the hip hurt more after the accident, but it is better now,' the doctor told her, then spoke again to their patient.

The strange language rattled around Meg's ears, and she wondered if this was how it would feel to be deaf. She knew people were speaking, yet she was totally isolated from their thoughts and ideas, cut off by the barrier of language as surely as she would be if she couldn't hear them at all.

Mrs Shagisi was holding one hand over her mouth, then expostulating loudly, from the sound of things. Her countryman nodded, then turned back to Meg.

'Also, she says she had a bad cold before she took the day trip and thought she might be getting the flu. She wore a mask on the bus, but no one has given her a mask in hospital.'

Meg remembered seeing photographs of Japanese

cities, and of people walking down the street with neat white masks over the mouth and nose.

'It's a good idea to stop the spread of infection, but it's not an Australian custom,' she explained. She thought for a minute, before adding, 'Maybe that explains the temperature. It could be a virus she picked up before she came in, and the antibiotics wouldn't touch it anyway.'

Meg felt relieved that one problem might be solved, although the difficulties of treating her Japanese patients would continue while they remained in hospital.

'How much time can you spend with us?' she asked the doctor, realising how important his co-operation would be.

'I will stay today and tonight, and after that I will leave my mobile-phone number. I will make sure you or the other staff can contact me at any time. If you have a problem, then I will talk to the patient as well as to you or any other doctor.'

'That's very kind of you,' Meg said, leading him back to the ward and up to the next of the new patients. 'I will arrange for you to meet the hospital translator. Maybe he could also contact you if he is confused by any of the medical terms we use.'

Together they checked on all the tourists in the orthopaedic ward, and Meg, surprised at first by the formality of the greetings between the Japanese, soon found herself bowing to the patients as she approached their beds. Was it lack of sleep that made the situation seem like a bizarre dream? she wondered, smiling and bowing with her physical body, while her mind rioted off at tangents.

'Would you like a cup of tea or coffee?' she asked

when the last query had been answered, and the last bow performed.

'Coffee, please, unless you have green tea,' Dr Sasaki responded with a grin.

'No green tea, and the coffee's not that marvellous,' Meg told him, ushering him into the small staff-room. 'And that brings us to another problem. What about food for all these patients? We don't want to upset their recovery by forcing on them food they can't eat.'

'All taken care of,' a voice replied, and she spun around to see Kate Allen, the hospital dietician, come through the door behind them, a young, petite and extremely beautiful Japanese woman behind her. 'Meet Mizaho,' Kate said. 'The travel company has given her to me for the duration. We have already spoken to all your patients and asked their preferences, and now we're going to work out a few menus for each of them. Once we've done that—'

She stopped abruptly, and Meg became aware of a peculiar quality to the silence that followed.

Kate was looking at Mizaho, who was staring, transfixed, at the doctor. He had also lapsed into a trance-like state, and the air in the small room throbbed with a strange vibrancy.

Oh, no! Meg thought, recognising immediately the insane, illogical, inexplicable attraction that had smitten these two people the moment they met. Just so had she and Jonathon stood when the lecture had ended long, long ago, and they had filed from the room—coming face to face in the doorway and stopping as suddenly as if they had hit a brick wall. Memories she didn't want to face forced themselves up from her subconscious. That first meeting! That first touch, when a fiery heat like nothing she had ever experienced or imagined had consumed her body.

'—we can repeat the menus if necessary. Lack of variety is better than unacceptable food,' Kate finished quietly then turned to Meg and added in a whisper, 'Do you suppose they know each other from somewhere?'

'I shouldn't think so!' Meg replied, trying to ignore her own torments, 'and I wouldn't worry about whispering. My guess is they've been transported to another plane altogether and they don't know we're here. I'm making coffee. You want some?'

She spoke with a wry humour, but the little scene had brought back too many reminders of the past, and triggered little impulses in senses that were already spun into confusion by Jonathon's return.

The silence was broken by an excited chatter of Japanese as Mizaho and Dr Sasaki both spoke at once, laughed together, then, in perfect accord, reached out to take each other's arms and walk out through the door.

'Well, I'm glad you arranged your menus before the lightning bolt struck,' Meg remarked as she watched them go. 'And I hope he remembers there are patients in other wards who would like to see him.'

'I think they're reliable and conscientious people, the Japanese,' Kate responded, but her voice was tinged with concern. 'Mizaho has already been through the other wards—we started at the bottom and worked up. Maybe she's taking him down there now.'

'Maybe,' Meg said as she passed Kate a cup of steaming coffee and sat down in one of the easy-chairs. She didn't believe it for a moment. What that pair wanted was a quiet corner where they could look at each other in peace, and get over the shock of their instant attraction.

She was certain she would see them again in about half an hour—and only then because Dr Sasaki had struck her as efficient and eminently trustworthy. She suspected that dedication to duty was a national characteristic, in which case Mizaho would also be guilt stricken when she realised that something so personal had distracted her from her work.

'Is she going to help the kitchen staff with meal preparation?' Meg asked but, before Kate could reply, her pager buzzed. She was wanted up on the fifth floor. For the first time since she had returned to the hospital she wondered what had happened to the theatre lists for today. Usually some efficient administrator would defer all operations, slotting the patients in over the next few days.

'She's arranged for a Japanese chef from one of the local restaurants to come in and do that,' Kate told her as she drained the last of her coffee.

'That's great,' Meg said. 'Now, when they come back, would you find someone to take Dr Sasaki down to General Surgery? I'll get down there as soon as I can. And could you please explain to him that most of the simple fractures were admitted there when we ran out of beds in the orthopaedic ward?'

Would this seem haphazard to the foreign doctor? she wondered as she hurried away. Or would a group of Australian tourists end up scattered through a Japanese hospital in the same way? It would be interesting to see how other hospitals worked, she decided, surprising herself with the thought. She had never had an urge to travel. It had been Jonathon who had always been wanting to see all the wonders the world had to offer, impatient to experience more and more.

Did he still feel like that? With a strange pang, she

realised that she didn't know—but that she wanted to! Wanted to know that and so many other things about this new Jonathon. Did he still twirl a few pieces of the hair above his left ear when he was reading? Did he still love honey but hate jam?

'The ante-room to Theatre Three,' a nurse told her when she emerged from the lift. 'It's a big pow-wow of some kind.'

James Clarke, chief superintendent of the hospital, was obviously in charge, Meg realised when she saw who was gathered. Don Grayson was there, and Jack Weston, Matron and two senior theatre sisters, two registrars she thought belonged in Casualty and A and E, and Bill. He grinned at her, and she felt herself smiling back. It confirmed her belief that he was good, his coming back to work this afternoon when he could have stayed at home.

He shifted on the couch, making room for her to squeeze in, and the silence as she settled herself suggested they had been waiting for her.

'I want to congratulate you all on the way you handled last night's crisis. I was proud to see how smoothly things proceeded,' James began. 'I will pass on my thanks to all the staff in time, but you people were the spearhead of the campaign, and you all acquitted yourselves well.'

There were a few embarrassed murmurs round the room, and Meg recognised how much they all liked to be praised—herself included!

'I know you understand that the job isn't over yet, and all care must be taken to ensure speedy recoveries for all the tourists. Ask Administration for any extra help you need, and use the translators and Japanese specialists we have been able to provide.'

Something was bothering their usually unflappable leader, Meg realised as she listened with half an ear to what he was saying and tried to guess what might lie behind his spoken words.

She didn't have to wonder for long, as his switch from praise to questioning was overly abrupt.

'Now, what measures remain in place against MRSA?' he asked, turning to the head theatre sister.

With a touch of pride in her voice, the woman ran through their procedures, finishing with the observation that it was more than two months since there had been any staphylococcus aureus infection discovered in any hospital patient.

An approving nod greeted this statement.

'So what antibiotic prophylaxis are you using on surgical patients, Dr Groves?'

The question was shot at Meg with such vigour that she could only look at her boss in amazement, unable to reply for a moment.

'Normally penicillin, if the patient is not allergic to it.' He knew this but Meg could see now where he was heading. She spoke calmly and rationally, hoping to defuse the argument before it began. 'Last night, because of the situation and the language barriers, we were unable to discover if many of the patients had suffered adverse reactions to any drugs. On those unable to communicate with us we used cephalosporins, as they are far less likely to produce anaphylactic shock.'

'You didn't consider using vancomycin as a prophylaxis?' he snapped, and Meg sat back in her chair. She had had this argument with James before! Surely he wasn't going to pursue it again in front of other senior staff?

'No, I didn't,' she said, keeping her voice carefully neutral. 'All the medical and nursing staff are aware of a possible recurrence of MRSA, and will watch the patients carefully. If any infection occurs, and it usually will to some degree in at least thirty per cent of post-operative patients, we will do a culture. If it is a staph infection then that's the time to bring in vancomycin.'

'Only bring in the big guns when the small artillery has failed,' Bill joked, and Meg knew he was trying to lighten the tension that had spread through the room.

'And what if that's too late? If infection has already spread into damaged bone tissues? How many of the Japanese patients needed pins or other implantations?' James demanded to know, and Meg, ignoring the rhetorical questions, listed the operations that had been performed.

'And you all knew that there was an increased risk of MRSA occurring in these patients—'

'If it was still present in the hospital, and if all the new sterilising and disinfection techniques have failed,' Meg broke in. 'All the procedures were carried out promptly, without interruption, and that lessens the risk significantly. As Sister explained, we've been free of it for months, but all the staff are conscious of the possibility of its recurring. In Theatre we follow the most stringent controls on instruments and soiled material. In the wards we are on the lookout for the slightest indication that a patient might have become infected.'

'Prophylactic use of vancomycin could eliminate that risk,' James declared, not quite making it an order.

'And increase the possibility that our particular strain of staph will become resistant to it. At the moment, at least we've got something we can use to treat it, should it resurface. In many places the bacterium is outstripping science's ability to control it.'

Meg knew that everyone in the room—except James—agreed with her, but they were all secretly pleased it was she doing battle, not them. The medical world was a small one, and advancement and promotion relied on the goodwill of those above you on the ladder. And how badly would her dream of reaching the top in surgery at Shorehaven be affected if these arguments with her boss continued?

'Well, I'm making you responsible,' James growled. 'Who knows how rich and influential these foreigners might be? Imagine what could happen if one of them becomes seriously ill with a staph infection—in our hospital!'

Was that what was bothering him? Meg wondered. That one of their patients might be 'rich and influential'? She wanted to laugh, but the focus of the man's concern was too absurd for laughter—and she didn't want to antagonise him even more.

She watched as he walked stiffly from the room, followed by Matron at her most regal, then looked around at her colleagues.

'Thanks, friends!' she said drily.

'Well, Meg, you're the one who stood up to him about this last time,' Jack said with an uneasy smile. 'I agree with you but I wouldn't argue with him over it. What's more, you handle it much better than the rest of us could.'

It was false praise, and Meg knew it.

'And I'm a woman, so my career path isn't as important as yours,' Meg said, putting into words what he was really thinking.

'I didn't say that,' Jack objected, 'but I do have a

wife and four kids to feed, and I need the hospital work he gives me until I can get my private practice established.'

'And if you keep on being nice to him he'll give you a consultancy.' The words were poisonously sweet, but the machinations of hospital politics infuriated Meg, who saw the welfare of the patients as her primary goal, and believed that excellence should be the only basis for promotion.

'If you two would stop arguing, we should consider what is upsetting our esteemed leader,' Bill interrupted. 'That little lecture wasn't brought on by the fact that one of our overseas patients might pick up a staph infection. Something's bothering him, and whatever it is it can't be minor. He would never let a little thing ruffle his perfect manners. Yet he failed to say good morning to us when he left, and Matron wasn't allowed to speak at all!'

They all turned to Bill, heads bobbing in agreement, eyes questioning.

'Nurses seem to hear the gossip first,' Jack said, turning to the two sisters.

'The cleaners know more than we do,' they chorused.

'And the volunteer staff knows more than them,' Bill agreed. He turned to Don, who was staring out of the window as if trying to distance himself from the mildly seditious conversation. 'You know the old boy best; what would you say is the matter?'

'I'd say it's pretty bad, whatever it is, but right now I have a practice to run, and will not spend any further time in unprofitable speculation.'

His words broke up the meeting, and people bustled from the room, Bill walking with Meg back to the lifts.

' "Unprofitable" is the key word,' she said. 'It's got to be funding cuts or something like that. When the staph infection was rioting through the hospital he was more concerned about the cost of treating the infected patients than about the infection itself. That's another reason he objects to our using cephalosporins—they're so much more expensive than most other antibiotics.'

The lift doors opened and they stepped inside.

'He's a money man, all right,' Bill agreed, 'but he couldn't run as efficient and effective a hospital if he didn't feel personally accountable for every cent.'

They emerged on the fourth floor to find Dr Sasaki standing in front of the lifts. There was no sign of Mizaho, but Meg imagined she could see a slight softening of the doctor's handsome oriental features, and an added gleam in his dark eyes.

She introduced Bill, and was surprised to hear him greet Dr Sasaki in halting Japanese.

'Learned it at school and tried to keep up with it,' he explained with an embarrassed grin.

'Well, in that case, you can take over as tour guide, and I can go home. If Dr Sasaki hasn't visited the patients in other wards, take him through them. Once they are all done, you might go back to Mrs Shagisi and see if you can sort out an Australian substitute for whatever she usually takes for the flu. She might be more comfortable if we can treat that as well as her arm and hip.'

'You take orders easily from a woman?' Dr Sasaki asked Bill.

'From this woman, any time!' he joked, but Meg felt a flutter of unease.

'In Australia more than half the medical graduates are women,' she told the visitor.

'But a much smaller percentage specialise, Meg,' Bill added. 'You are something of a rarity.'

'And expendable, according to Jack,' she said crisply as the sexist remark made earlier echoed in her mind.

'No way!' Bill assured her, and led the other doctor away.

But was Jack right? Should promotion go to the person who had more responsibilities?

A wave of tiredness swept over her, and she thrust aside the thought. Time to go home, she decided— then she remembered her impetuous flight. Could she go home? It seemed stupid not to, she decided. Jonathon would be safely back in Brisbane, and she would sleep better in her own bed. She crossed to the phone, found the number and dialled the motel.

'. . .so I wondered if you could pack up my things and put them in a cab and send them to this address,' she was asking a moment later. She gave her home address, pleased that Mrs Edwards had heard about the accident and correctly assumed she had been held up at the hospital. 'If you put my account in the suit-case, I'll send you a cheque,' she added.

'Nonsense,' Mrs Edwards replied. 'You were hardly here at all. And we weren't so busy that we needed the room, not like tomorrow, being Saturday and all.'

Tomorrow was Saturday? Surely not! Meg said good-bye and hung up, forcing her mind to think—to work out where the week had gone.

If tomorrow was Saturday, she'd half promised Dave she would go out to dinner with him. Had he been trying to contact her?

And what of Jonathon? Would he come again? He had said he would! Unfinished business, he had said.

She lifted a hand and brushed her fingers across her lips.

Unfinished business! Her body trembled, but she steeled herself against the weakness. She didn't want to talk to Jonathon! Didn't want to dredge up all the old hurts, all the bitterness that had soured her life for so long.

Her thoughts clattered like cymbals in her head. What she needed was a good night's sleep, then some quiet, uninterrupted time to think things through.

And she had closed the door on her bolt-hole! She thought of the ward, but Gemma's room was no longer the sanctuary it had been.

She breathed deeply, calming nerves that were fluttering towards panic. She had to go home first, whatever else she did or didn't do. Any minute now there would be a cab on its way with her suitcase. She had to be there to meet it.

Once again, there was no sign of Jonathon's car outside her flat, and she told herself she was glad. Three hours' sleep in the last twenty-four was not a good basis for discussion of anything.

And what was there to discuss? A sexual compatibility that had survived its initial fiery birth, ignored all sense and reason, and held them together for far longer than their relationship should have lasted. Even four years apart had done little to dim its burning lustre if her physical reactions were anything to judge by.

She blushed in the fading light, and greeted the arrival of the taxi with relief. Unpacking, showering, washing her clothes, vacuuming, feeding herself— menial tasks performed mechanically, filling in time until she could go to bed and banish the nagging voices in her head with the oblivion of sleep.

Tonight, as she looked around her flat, the loneliness of her single life hit her for the first time. Her upbringing, as the quiet, clever eldest child of seven, had made her long for a time when she could live on her own, and she had set herself that goal when she had been very young. Then Jonathon had come along!

CHAPTER SEVEN

'MRS SHAGISI's temperature is down and she's far more comfortable today.'

The good news greeted her when she walked into the ward early next morning, determined to get her ward-round out of the way so that she could relax for the day. The sight of the duty sister sitting behind the desk was a confirmation that the staff were not experiencing any major dramas.

'And the other tourists?' Meg asked.

Sister Gilbert, an older woman who worked weekends by choice, gave a brief summary of each patient's condition, and Meg made mental notes of the ones who might need special attention.

'Mr Rogers' daughter came in,' Sister added. 'I told her we'd see about getting him a pronged stick. She would like to take him home with her on Tuesday.'

From the sound of her voice, Sister Gilbert didn't agree with this plan, Meg realised. She waited while the nurse explained.

'I think she figures if she gets him there while his movement is still restricted he might find himself enjoying her place by the time he's well enough to leave.' Disapproval of this management plan dripped from the words.

'I suppose I'll feel happier about discharging him if I know he'll have someone to look after him for a while, but once he's fully mobile, and can care for himself, he should be allowed to choose where he wants to live,' Meg agreed. 'I suppose it might be more convenient for his daughter to have him where she can keep an eye on him, but he's entitled to a choice.'

The other woman sighed, and shook her head. 'Why is it that the elderly people who can't care for themselves and want to go and live with their children are rarely wanted, and those who don't are frequently forced into it?'

'Life's never neat and tidy, that's why,' Meg told her. 'And it's often a question of the timing being all wrong.' Perhaps it was timing that had wrecked her relationship with Jonathon, a hopeful voice whispered in her head. But would now be any better? 'You can't blame a woman with three pre-schoolers being reluctant to take on the care of an invalid parent as well. There are situations where it's impossible.'

She forced herself to concentrate on Sister Gilbert's concerns.

'I know you're right, but I can't help worrying about some of the patients we send home to unsatisfactory situations. Remember Mrs Short?'

The conversation twisted through past patients, and Meg shifted uneasily as she watched the clock tick away precious minutes of her day off. Last week's Meg would not have minded stopping to talk, she realised, and the thought made her more attentive to the sister's complaints, in spite of a growing urge to escape to some quiet corner where she could try to sort out her emotional chaos.

'Who else is going home?' she asked, to divert the conversation back to practical matters. 'Will we have enough beds for the new patients after surgery sessions on Monday and Wednesday?'

She watched as the sister flicked through her notes.
'Three of the Japanese are leaving today. The travel
company has arranged private nursing in their hotel
rooms. How many on your Monday list?'

Meg thought for a moment. 'There are two hip
replacements and a shoulder reconstruction that I can
remember,' she said. 'And I think a hand contracture
that could have been day surgery but the patient is
diabetic, so I need to keep an eye on her. I'd like to
put the diabetic woman and the man who's having
acromioplasty into single rooms. Shoulders are always
very painful and the diabetic woman will need extra
attention.'

'Could we shift Gemma back to kids'?'

The question stunned Meg for a moment, then she
began to wonder if perhaps that should be the next
logical move for the little girl, especially if she was
going to be sent to a foster family who already had
other children. Wouldn't it be better to break her in to
children's company within the security of the hospital
environment?

Again the thought of Gemma's departure tugged at
her heart, but Sister was waiting for her reply.

'See if they have a spare bed in a two-bed room.
That would be better than the ward. If they have a
suitable bed, we can talk to her about it, but all the
staff will have to co-operate, emphasising how great it
will be for her to be with other kids.'

They were still discussing the problem when Mark
arrived.

'Working weekends now?' Meg asked.

He shook his head. 'Pleasure this time. I'm taking
Gemma home for the weekend. My mum is visiting
and she wants to go to Sea World and Movieworld and

all the other touristy attractions, so I thought Gemma might as well come along.'

'What a great idea!' Meg felt relief wash away the subconscious guilt that thoughts of Gemma had been causing. 'I'll pop in and see her first; then you can be on your way. We've been talking about shifting her to a two-bed kids' room. Sister is about to ring and find out what's available. If there's room there, will you talk to her about it over the weekend?'

She smiled appealingly at Mark, knowing she was pushing the responsibility for telling Gemma on to his shoulders.

Mark grinned, and nodded. 'But you'll owe me one huge favour,' he told her. 'And don't expect me to forget!'

She followed him into Gemma's room.

'Have a lovely weekend, little one,' she murmured to the delighted child. 'I'll see you Monday.'

Hurrying back to the ward, she visited her patients, pausing to speak to each one.

'Bill's on call this weekend, and he'll be in tomorrow,' she told the sister as she made her way to the lifts.

'So I finally catch up with you!'

Dave stood directly in front of her, his solid, bulky figure gradually revealed as the lift doors slid open. Her body should have responded in some way, she realised, if he was ever going to be anything more than a friend!

She smiled at him, but the movement of her lips was forced, and her legs stiffly reluctant as she stepped in to stand beside him.

'You heard about the coach crash,' she offered feebly.

'That and other things,' he muttered. 'Can you spare the time for a cup of coffee?'

'Of course I can,' she said, but heard her own uneasiness underpinning the words as the lift stopped on the ground floor and he led the way out.

She followed him to the canteen, waited while he bought their coffee, then walked with him across the courtyard to the most secluded corner.

'I know you said you didn't want to get involved,' he began as she reached for the sugar, 'but you let me think it was because of the pressure of work; because you felt you hadn't the time to invest in a relationship. You might have mentioned you were already married.'

He sounded so aggrieved that Meg forgot her annoyance with Jonathon and his lie, and bit back a wry smile. Had Dave thought, in spite of her warning, that he would woo her and win her?

'I'm not married,' she told him firmly, 'and I don't want to be. I'm not saying not ever, but definitely not yet.'

Dave's blue eyes narrowed as he frowned across the table at her.

'That lawyer chap who's hanging round the hospital says you're married to him,' he argued.

'And as he's a fellow male, his word must be gospel? I am not married to Jonathon Prior and never have been.' The words came out crisp and cold but her mind veered away from the problems the rumour-mill would cause. The description Dave had used clanged in her head. 'What do you mean by "hanging round the hospital"?'

The fair head tilted, and she saw his gaze move over her face, as if he was reassessing her.

'He was here most of yesterday,' he growled. 'Seems

we're to become another America with ambulance-
chasing lawyers persuading clients to litigate!'

Shock slammed through Meg's body. Jonathon
would never do a thing like that! Never, never, never!
Not the Jonathon she'd known—the man she had
loved to distraction.

'Is this another rumour racing through the corridors
or did you actually see him on the premises?' She
bit out the words, curt and waspish, but doubt had
catapulted her mind into total chaos and the prospect
of such betrayal was making her feel physically ill.

'I've seen him around,' Dave confirmed. 'And why
did he say he was married to you if it's not true?'

Meg shrugged. 'I don't know,' she said tiredly. 'We
knew each other once but it was long ago. I'm
sorry, Dave.'

'Sorry he's saying it, or sorry you didn't tell me, or
sorry that now he's back you don't want to go out with
me any more?'

She bent her head and twirled the teaspoon in the
muddy-looking froth in the bottom of her coffee-cup.
She could blot out the hurt look in Dave's eyes, but
she couldn't ignore the bitterness in his voice.

'I'm sorry you heard the rumour; sorry if it upset
you,' she said carefully, pushing the froth into meaningless patterns.

'Well, I'm sorry too!' he stormed and she heard the
scrape of his chair being pushed back and looked up
in time to see him stride away, past her shoulder,
heading towards the door.

Was it her over-stimulated imagination or did he
mutter 'ambulance chaser' as he departed? She
shrugged again, and concentrated fiercely on the
puddle in her coffee-cup.

'Trying to read your future in the leaves?' The sound of Jonathon's voice tightened every sinew in her body.

'It's coffee!' she mumbled dejectedly as he dropped into the recently vacated chair. 'What are you doing here?'

She didn't—couldn't!—look up, apprehension freezing her muscles into painful immobility.

'If I said looking for you, would you believe me?' he asked.

'It would be the best of a bad choice,' she muttered. 'Not exactly welcome but infinitely preferable to the alternative.'

She saw his hand reach out across the table, and straightened as his fingers touched the skin beneath her chin.

'Which is?' he probed, his green eyes impaling her with their penetrating scrutiny.

'A tout,' she muttered in despair. 'Someone looking for business. An "ambulance chaser", as they're called in America.' She watched him closely as she spoke, and saw his lips tighten.

'Could you believe that of me?' he asked, the words crisped by anger. 'Is it possible that, knowing me, you even feel the need to ask?'

'I've had plenty of time to wonder if I ever knew you,' she pointed out. 'I didn't think the Jonathon I knew would insist on going back to England just when my training position was offered. I couldn't believe, in spite of the problems we'd been having, my career, my future would mean so little to you.'

Was it because she knew his face so well that she saw the pain that shadowed it, or would the unmistakable quiver of anguish have been obvious to anyone?

'Jonathon!' She cried his name, her body responding

automatically, her hand reaching out to cover his, her fingers squeezing tightly. For a moment, his hand returned the pressure, then he shrugged and withdrew his hand.

'Have you heard the rumour that I've been in Antarctica?' He followed the bizarre question with a smile of sorts, a crooked twisting of his lips that told her he had changed the subject deliberately. The door, so briefly opened, had been closed, shutting her out.

She was puzzled and upset, but allowed herself to be diverted. 'Antarctica? What would a lawyer have been doing in Antarctica?'

He shrugged and smiled again, a warm, conspiratorial grin. 'Chasing ambulances, perhaps?'

'I suppose it's just as likely,' she admitted, answering his smile with a rueful grin. 'But you've certainly switched the hospital gossip machine into overdrive with that absurd marriage statement.'

'And upset you?' he asked huskily, his voice deepened with concern.

Meg shook her head, and met his questing gaze defiantly. 'Rumours and gossip have never worried me in the slightest, you know that,' she assured him, then wondered why she felt the need to ease his mind. He'd caused her so much trouble that she should be trying to upset him, not consoling him. Was it because she'd seen that fleeting instant of pain?

'The boyfriend looked bothered.' His eyes reflected the challenge and she tried to outglare him, but her eyelids fluttered and dropped while heat zoomed into her cheeks.

'He didn't. . . Dave's not. . . He's a friend!' Her blustering reply infuriated her. How could he reduce her to a stammering mess after all this time? 'Not that

it's any of your business,' she added frostily, hoping
to make up lost ground.

'Of course not,' he said cheerfully, then he stood
up, bent forward to drop a kiss on the top of her head,
and added, 'Well, I'd better go chase an ambulance!'
and walked away.

Meg turned, staring after him in dismay. How could
he still affect her this way? And why did it seem as if
he was flirting with her? She stood up and walked
slowly out of the hospital, puzzling over his behaviour.
It wasn't until she was at the front gate that she realised
she hadn't thought about the one question that should
be worrying her—the question of his presence in the
hospital.

'If you're free tomorrow, would you come climb a
mountain with me? For old times' sake and because I
badly need some exercise. I'll come by later or you
could ring me on. . .' The number was the mobile one
Jonathon had given the other night.

It was the only message on her answering machine,
and it infuriated her. If he wanted to invite her out—
'for old times' sake'—why hadn't he asked her when
he had seen her in the canteen? Even if he'd phoned
before he had seen her, he could have mentioned he'd
left a message.

She tried to follow his thought processes, to work
out why the clever man had done things this way, but
the task defeated her. How could she second-guess a
stranger?

He'd come by later, would he? she thought angrily.
And would he expect her to be waiting patiently for
his arrival?

'We'll see about that!' she muttered at the answering

machine, then grabbed her handbag and keys and headed out of the flat. She'd go shopping, that was what she'd do! And if he 'came by' he would find her gone and have to take himself away again.

She strode up the road, her feet pounding on the pavement to the same angry tempo as her thoughts. Rage at his presumption—his persistence—carried her into the supermarket, but as she propelled a trolley mindlessly down the aisles she found her fingers reaching for nuts and dried fruit, for chocolate bars and barley sugar—the nibbling food they'd always carried on their climbing expeditions.

I can't want to go! her mind wailed, but she knew she did, and probably would.

Jonathon drove with the casual ease he brought to most tasks, and Meg was content to simply sit and let the world pass by. There were questions she could ask, like where were they going, and where was he living, and why had he come back to Australia, but she didn't want to know the answer to any of them enough to break the companionable silence that had settled between them.

They crossed the river, bypassing the centre of Brisbane, and headed north, following a broad highway to where dark green pine plantations began to close in on either side of the road. When he took the turn-off to Beerburrum her heart leapt with a gladness that was only partly to do with the company. She loved the queer misshapen mountains they called the Glasshouses, loved the challenge of climbing their steep slabs of rock, of reaching the top and surveying the land beneath with an immeasurable satisfaction.

'Do you still climb?' he asked, breaking into her thoughts with uncanny accuracy.

'I haven't for ages,' she replied. Not since you left and took away the fun of it, she added silently.

He drove along the old road north until they reached the foot of the big, ape-like mountain, Tibrogargan. Here he turned onto an unsealed forestry road, following its rough course towards the camping site they had always used.

'Can we talk about what happened to us? Before I had to. . .decided to go back to England?' he asked, his eyes on the road and his profile gravely set.

Meg looked away from it, out at the bleached white trunks of the eucalypts that lined the road. So he did want to talk!

She thought about it then realised she could finally put aside the bitterness and blame that had clouded the issues in her mind for too long. Slowly, and hesitantly, she began, voicing embryonic thoughts.

'We were such different people. For the first two years of our relationship the differences didn't matter, because what we did have was overwhelming everything else.'

'For the first two years I was studying medicine with you,' he pointed out.

Arrested by the dryness in his voice, she glanced at him, but his face was giving nothing away.

'Do you think things changed because I resented your wanting to complete your law degree?'

He didn't answer, his whole being seemingly focused on turning the car off the road and down a narrow track towards a fresh, sparkling creek. Meg wound down her window and listened to the sounds of the bush. Soft winds rustled the leaves on the trees, birds called to one another, and the water chuckled its way over stones.

'I didn't,' she added. 'Not consciously, anyway. I wanted you to be happy, Jonathon.'

'But happy in your world!'

A hardness in the words made her swing away from the quiet magic of the bush beyond the car, and stare at him in amazement. Sun streamed through the window, burnishing his hair, and back-lighting his face.

'Not our world?' she asked quietly. She reached out and brushed the back of her hand down his cheek, but he neither flinched nor softened. 'I always thought of it that way, although I know my work commitments and my family nearly drove you mad at times.'

She paused for a moment, searching for the words she wanted. 'That's one of the things I couldn't understand. You seemed to resent my family, yet you were so determined to have children of your own.'

'And you, who leapt into the fray every time one of your sisters or brothers asked for something, seemed to think you had enough dependants in your life,' he countered.

She looked at him, trying to see back to the man he'd been four years earlier.

'I wondered, afterwards, if it had been some kind of test—asking me to have your child,' she said quietly. 'You liked to challenge me, to set me up and watch which way I'd jump.'

He half smiled now, and shook his head. 'But you always knew, or guessed when I was doing it,' he challenged. 'And you delighted in beating me at my own game, deliberately choosing a position that would mislead me.'

'Until it stopped being a game.' The words eased

off her lips, hardly louder than a sigh, but with them came the pain and loneliness of four years' absence, and unaccustomed tears made her blink quickly and turn away.

'Until it stopped being a game!' he echoed. The deep despair in his voice coiled its way into her heart, filling it with an aching heaviness.

'And is rehashing old hurts what you wanted to do?' she croaked. 'Is this the talk we had to have?'

Green eyes gleamed down at her. 'Maybe we need to hurt before we can heal,' he suggested. 'Just as you surgeons debride all the dead tissue from a wound, maybe we need to do that with our emotions.'

Something hung suspended in the air between them, some hidden meaning, some clue Meg could not grasp.

'What do you mean?' she whispered, not at all certain that she wanted to know the answer.

'I mean this, Meggie,' he said, leaning across the space between the seats to kiss her softly on the lips, 'And this,' he added, moving his lips to blow warmth into her ear, 'and this.' His hand reached out and touched her shoulder, sending her blood into a further frenzy, but she already had the message. Whatever it was between them, it had not been killed by their arguments and fury, nor lessened by the four long years apart.

'It's lust, Jonathon,' she gasped as his lips closed in on hers once more. 'It's a transient physical thing,' she mumbled against the soft, seductive kisses.

'Physical, but hardly transient, my love,' he murmured, teasing her to a trembling fervour with tiny nibbling kisses against the soft skin of her neck. 'I waited four years for it to lessen, for my hunger for you to die or go away. Then I realised it wouldn't and packed my bags.'

His lips had reached the skin above the buttons on her shirt, and Meg's body stiffened, holding itself taut as it waited, and longed, and hoped. Keep touching me, she wanted to shout, her mind beyond responding to his confession—wanting, needing, demanding the pleasure that only Jonathon could give.

'Perhaps we should go climb a mountain,' he muttered, lifting his head so that he could look down into her eyes, 'before things get out of hand.'

His breathing had a ragged urgency, and his green eyes blazed with the hunger he had mentioned earlier.

The fires of desire flared higher and higher, and Meg knew she no longer wanted to fight them. Did it matter that it was only lust? Couldn't that appetite, like greed, be satisfied occasionally?

'Or we could forget the mountain and stay here,' she suggested and saw his face grow pale.

'I didn't whisk you off to spend the day seducing you in the front seat of a car, Meg,' he growled. 'If that was all I wanted, we would have been much more comfortable at home in a proper bed.'

'Then what do you want?' she whispered, so caught up in the web of the other wanting that the words trembled on her lips.

'I want to see if there's a way for us to be together again; to start over with a more solid foundation so we can build a future together.'

The words hung in the air between them, promising so much that Meg could scarcely breathe. But the intimations they brought with them—an end to the emptiness, the loneliness she had felt for four years— were an illusion, she knew that. She and Jonathon had

tried once before and failed. What had changed that
would make a second try more likely to succeed?

'We've both matured,' he said, replying so precisely
to her unspoken question that shock jolted through
her. 'We're no longer students or first-year slaves, and
we're settled in our respective careers. Our lives are
more orderly, more able to be fitted together without
constant friction and disruption.'

Meg watched his face as he spoke, and saw, behind
the earnestness, a trace of fear. She recognised it
because it mirrored her own feelings. Were they both
afraid that this was the last throw of the dice? Afraid
because they knew if they tried and failed again they
would be cut off from each other forever?

'You make us sound like bits of an engine that need
to be fitted together,' she murmured as lightly as she
could, while a growing panic welled up within her. Did
she want to start again, to experience the bliss
and rapture of that closeness, to grow used again to
his presence in her bed, the male smell of him in
rooms he'd recently left? And could she risk the pain
of failure if they hadn't matured enough? If it didn't
work out?

Make a joke of it, Meg, she told herself, keep it light!

'And I thought that was the bit that worked!' she
added, with a lascivious wink.

A smile eased the taut lines of his face.

'Out, woman,' he ordered. 'Let's go climb a mountain. Maybe that will cool your ardour enough for us
to have a rational conversation.'

'You started the kissing,' she reminded him as she
pushed open the car door. She loved climbing, and
her body needed the exercise, yet she couldn't banish
a feeling of apprehension.

Jonathon had obviously been thinking about this 'getting back together' notion for some time—at least as long as it had taken to finalise his business commitments in England and re-establish himself in Australia. Also, he was a lateral thinker, one who would canvas all the broader issues, but trained to marshal his arguments so they could be presented in the most persuasive manner.

She, on the other hand, had not—except in wild imaginings and errant dreams—ever considered the possibility that she would see him again, let alone contemplate living with him! And, now she had to think about it, could she risk being hurt again? Would she have to reconsider marriage? Was that what he still wanted? A sense of being put at an unfair disadvantage stirred a fitful anger. She shut the car door with a little slam.

'Shall I take the blanket?' he asked. 'We could have a sleep in the sun up on top.'

On top? Up where they had pledged their love? Back then, the silent dawn bush had been their witness, and a fiery sun had risen above the horizon and added its radiant benediction of warmth and light.

'No!' she replied, not wanting to remember, not willing to relive that particular bit of the past.

'Or I could take the little tent,' he tempted, but the thought of what he wanted her to decide had killed the twirling torment of passion—for a time, at least.

'I thought talking was the main item on your agenda,' she told him tartly, striding off towards the narrow track that would lead them to the base of the mountain.

Did she want to try again? The question pursued her, but how could she produce a rational answer?

Her body longed for his touch, her mind sought the intellectual challenge of their debates, and instinct told her she was not meant to live alone, yet the enormity of their failure and his determined departure was like a thick black curtain, blotting out the faintest ray of hope that it might work a second time around.

Twigs snapping behind her told her he was catching up, and she hurried on, not wanting his physical closeness to disrupt the few brain cells she had managed to press into action.

'If you're going to maintain this breakneck pace, stop at the bottom of the first of the high slabs. We'll rope up there to be on the safe side.'

She nodded, but kept going, climbing now, stepping carefully through the loose rocks that littered the lower slopes of the mountain.

Around her, the tall gums were giving way to wattle and banksia, and blackboys, the strange stunted grasstrees of the Australian bush, brought a brighter green to the silver-grey of the bush. If they got back together, need it fail? That was the question she had to answer because she knew she couldn't live through losing him again.

She pulled herself up the first small cliff, and sank onto a sunwarmed rock. Below her to the north, the scrub gave way to a pineapple farm, neat rows of pale, serrated spikes marching across the slope of the foothills.

Beyond the farm, other mountains jutted up from the plain—Coonowrin, Beerburrum, and Ngun Ngun, strong, solid shapes thrusting their summits towards the blue sky.

'Beautiful as ever!' Jonathon sighed, dropping down beside her. 'I thought of this so often, in the end I

had to come back to see if it had been real.' He reached
out, so casually, and draped his arm across her shoulder, then kissed her cheek—affectionately!

Was 'this' this place, Meg wondered, or their
togetherness? But a wonderful contentment stole over
her before she could find an answer, so she dropped
her head against his shoulder and stopped thinking
altogether.

'If we could respect each other's careers and our
right to pursue them, and learn to fit in with each
other's timetables, it would be a good base,' he said
quietly. 'And if we could try to define what we each
want from the relationship, and meet each other on
those things, then that's the next step conquered.
Surely we're mature enough now to negotiate the
differences?'

Meg looked out at the blue sky, staring into its
infinite distance until her eyes hurt. He made it sound
so logical, he raised hope to expectancy, yet doubt still
simmered strongly inside her, buoyed up by her fear
of the pain of failure.

She said nothing, and, in time, he continued, his
voice low and serious.

'If we can eradicate petty annoyances, then tension
won't build up between us, Meg. With common sense
and planning, surely that's possible!'

He had certainly thought things through, and now
he spoke as if it was all settled!

'It wasn't only the little things we disagreed on,
Jonathon.' Meg bit out the words, angry with his insistence that they spoil her peace and contentment with
talk, especially talk that was so tantalising. 'You said
it yourself. It was also our thoughts, ideas, ideals and
dreams—fundamental things like that. And now our

careers—at odds with each other by their diverse natures.'

'Not necessarily,' he assured her. 'I can defend doctors and hospitals as easily as I can defend their patients.'

'But would you, if a patient needed you to defend them?'

He didn't answer for a moment and Meg found herself holding her breath.

'You would have to trust me to choose cases that could not clash with your position. And isn't trust what love is all about?'

She felt his body relaxing, and his hand rubbing tenderly against her arm. Tremors of excitement started in the skin beneath his touch, rippling outwards through her body like waves across a lake.

'Trust me, Meggie,' he murmured, his lips pressing against the top of her head.

The tremors becoming jolting currents. How could she think when a touch, a few murmured words, turned her bones to jelly?

Her head nodded against his arm, and her body filled with the bittersweet heaviness of desire. She felt him move, then his head blotted out the sun and his lips met hers, teasing at the contours of her mouth.

'I love you, Meg,' he whispered, his breath a caress that lingered on her lips. And now his hands were inside her shirt, holding the weight of breasts that ached for more than he was giving. 'Do you love me?'

She tried to reply, but now one hand had slipped between her legs, feeling through tough bush clothes her ready, eager softness.

She moaned against his mouth, her own hands scrabbling with his buttons, needing skin on skin, the feel of bone, and warmth, and heartbeats. Zips were unzipped, buttons popped, clothes sloughed off with awkward urgency, then he was lifting her, turning her towards him, drawing her up high onto his thighs. With a tenderness that belied their haste he eased her moist, aching flesh down and down until he was so deep inside her that she groaned with the pleasure of it.

'Would getting pregnant matter?' he whispered in her ear as they paused for a moment to savour the uniqueness of their union.

'I suppose it would,' Meg muttered, so deeply lost in pleasurable sensations that she was dismayed that he would spoil it with such a mundane consideration. Of course it would, you stupid woman! her mind shouted, but her lips refused to move again.

'Then I'll be careful,' he told her, and held her hard against his chest, moving only enough to start the rippling springs of her pleasure while keeping his own release in check. 'I hadn't planned a halfway-up seduction.'

Meg moved her head, capturing his lips with hers, although she found his matter-of-fact conversation nearly as stimulating as his teasing hands and subtle body movements.

She twisted on his lap and stiffened, feeling the bonelessness of climax shuddering through to her toes.

'You planned all this; did you plan precautions?' she mumbled when the glory faded enough for words to come again.

He held her close, anchoring her to him, as if her pleasure was his one desire.

'I did, with a kind of mad hope, but I can wait till later. I've done my thinking about our future, Meggie; I know what I want.'

She looked into his eyes and saw his love and commitment. But he had always had that for her—until he'd gone away! Leaving her alone and hurting so badly that she had wondered if she would survive. She slid away from him, pulling on her clothes with a feverish urgency.

Had he made love to her to help some agenda of his own? Was he controlled enough to have done that deliberately—even denying himself, while ensuring she was satisfied?

She shook her head, not knowing any more. It was all part of the mystery that was this new Jonathon!

CHAPTER EIGHT

YELLOW marks showed the easiest way up the rock slab, and Jonathon went ahead, securing pitons in crevices and playing out the rope to Meg. Experienced climbers would race up without ropes, but being cautious was better than being dead—that was one thing on which they had always agreed!

She looked up, seeing his strong legs above her on the slab, knowing the shape of him from this angle so well that it was like seeing her own shadow. Her heart ached for the blissful years of the past, while her mind wondered about his behaviour on the rock ledge below.

Had that seduction and sacrifice scene been part of an overall plan? Jonathon might have seemed impulsive—even wild—to others, but she knew his quick brain was always thinking ahead, working out the next few moves in what might appear to be fateful happenings.

At the top, the coastline wove its pattern of green and gold and blue. The long low island that was Bribie divided the glittering waters of the passage from the white-flecked ocean. Civilisation spread across one corner of the island, and huge tower blocks reared on the mainland to the north, but in between were pine forests, and grey native scrub, then the dense green of mangrove swamps where the water seeped into the edge of the continent.

'Beautiful!' Jonathon breathed, then he turned to Meg and his eyes repeated the message. Reaching out,

138

he took her hand, then led her to a rocky outcrop where they could sit and drink in the splendour of the scene spreading beneath them.

'Could we start again?' he asked at last, his eyes on the curled horizon.

Meg's body tightened, wanting what he offered, both now and for the immediate future, but her mind remained obtusely blank, unwilling to say yes, but unable to muster one single logical argument against it. Except that it hadn't worked before!

'I'd like to try,' he offered.

'And if it doesn't work, if I can't agree with what you want to do, would you walk away again?' she asked.

'I had to go,' he said quietly, and the words reverberated down into her soul.

She felt her brow pucker into a frown. 'I had to go.' He had said that more than once before, yet she'd never asked why! Was now the time?

'Had to go?' she repeated.

He turned towards her, and she saw the pain again.

'My mother had cancer,' he said quietly.

'Mother? Cancer? You have a mother?'

A rueful smile greeted her incredulous gasps, then he added gravely, 'Had a mother! She died three months ago.'

'Honestly, Jonathon! What kind of a relationship did we have?' Meg demanded, shattered by the revelations. 'First you have a mother you let me think was dead, then, when you decide to go back to England because she's dying, you refuse to tell me that's the reason and leave me believing it was some wayward whim. And you talk about trust!'

She threw her hands in the air and shook her head in utter disbelief. 'Did you think I wouldn't want to go with you? Wouldn't want to be with you and support you and help you all I could?' she demanded.

He reached out and grabbed her flailing arms, slipping his hands down them until he caught her fingers in his.

'Of course I knew you'd want to be with me!' he growled. 'That's one of the reasons I didn't tell you. You'd just been offered the chance of a lifetime with that place on the orthopaedic programme. If I had told you why I had to go and you'd given up that opportunity, how would you have felt later?'

'You could have let me decide that!' she argued hotly. 'At least given me the choice!'

He bent towards her so that he could look into her eyes.

'And if you'd made the choice to go with me and then regretted it? What hope would there have been for a future together?'

She twisted her hands out of his grasp and turned away, unable to reply. At the time of his departure they had begun to realise that love did not conquer all and tension between them had been stretched to breaking point. As their relationship had developed, binding them into a single, inter-dependent unit, they had both panicked, each fighting for a separate identity within their relationship. In such a fragile emotional climate, could he have told her?

'And your mother?' she asked, turning away from the painful memories and unanswerable questions.

'I hadn't known she was alive,' he said slowly. 'My parents split up when I was eight months old, and, as my mother was content for my father to raise me, they decided it would be less hurtful for me if I was told she had died.'

Dismay and disbelief jangled in Meg's head, but Jonathon was speaking again and she concentrated on his words.

'When she was diagnosed as having breast cancer and found she had only a short time to live she contacted my father.' He paused and she heard the air rasp into his lungs. 'She wanted to see me, but the decision was to be mine. She said she would understand if I didn't want to contact her.'

His voice faded away, and he turned to look out over the view, but she knew he was not seeing the beauty. The crease in his cheek had deepened and beneath his jaw a muscle quivered.

'I would have come with you and not regretted it!' Meg cried, hoping to ease the agony she could see in his face.

'Would you, Meg? Could you have been certain of that?' A bird soared above them, crying into the silence, but Meg did not reply, sensing Jonathon had more to add.

'They had loved each other so much, my father said, but she had regretted getting married. Regretted the pregnancy, then the burden of having a child. He told me this when he told me she was alive, and sick, and asking for me. Could I tell you that, use it to persuade you to come with me, knowing what sadness love had brought to them both? Knowing that regrets had torn them apart and would possibly do the same to us?'

'But you asked me to go with you anyway!' she objected bitterly. 'You made it a kind of test! If I had gone with you, not knowing the reason you had to go, it would prove I loved you.'

'I hoped you'd trust me enough to know I wouldn't

go unless I had to,' he muttered. 'That was vanity,
I know.'

He shrugged, then turned back to face her
once again.

'Maybe I was wrong, but I was so confused, Meg.
At the time it seemed as if my life had been built on
lies—as if I would never be able to trust anyone again.
Maybe what I wanted was for you to prove me wrong.'

His voice was hoarse with the heartache of the past.

'And, even when you said no, I knew I had to go,
to be with the woman who had given birth to me, then
walked away. She was asking for me, Meg!'

Tears for the woman she had not known welled up
inside her, and questions fought to be asked. Did she
suffer much? Were you with her all the time? Are you
glad you went? But the lump in her throat made it
impossible to speak and she turned to him, moving into
his opening arms like a straying child returning home.

'We lost four years!' she murmured when the tears
were gone, and the passionate kisses that had followed
them had eased most of the pain.

'Lost and gained,' he assured her. 'Maybe they were
years we both needed to finish growing up, to get our
separate lives in order before we could embark on a
joint venture.'

She felt him smile as his lips pressed against her
cheek, and smiled herself, knowing he was right. For
two hours they talked, making plans, settling on ways
to handle this, to avoid that, to reach compromises
before tension stretched so tightly between them that
words were no longer possible.

'Not quite the vows we made last time,' he said,
grinning at her with the wry, lopsided smile that turned
her knees to water.

'Last time we were young enough to believe that the mystical ideals like love and honour would transcend everything, overcoming all obstacles, leaping all barriers,' she reminded him.

'And so they should,' he whispered against her ear, sealing the tentative beginning with moth-soft touches of his lips against her skin.

Kisses killed the plans, for a while at least, but when he released her again, and spoke of settling in Shorehaven, finding a bigger flat, together, a subtle shading in his voice pierced the iridescent fog that was her brain.

'There might be a big case coming up there shortly,' he said, his voice easy and relaxed now that the major decision of their new togetherness had been reached.

Meg, resting back against his chest, heard the words, but they didn't do more than ripple across the surface of her strange contentment.

'It's to do with the trouble you mentioned at the hospital,' he added, so casually that again she failed to hear a premonition of disaster. 'Seems someone decided to sue over a Golden Staph infection he contracted there, and some hot-shot lawyer is scouting around trying to find more people who have been affected to bring a class action for negligence against the hospital.'

The coldness started in her chest, as if her heart had frozen to a solid block of ice with splinters reaching through her blood vessels to immobilise her body.

Was this his reason for seeking a reconciliation? How could he chat so casually about such a case? Could he not see how it would affect her? Not realise that court action against her hospital was an action against her?

The heaviness that weighted her to the ground was

no longer the heaviness of love, but of dread, of disbelief—of pain, and endings, and despair.

'You wouldn't take it!' she croaked, forcing the words out of her dry throat, begging him to laugh and say he was teasing.

'It would be a fantastic case to fight, Meg,' he replied, all enthusiasm. Couldn't he feel her coldness? Didn't he know her love was dying in his arms? 'It would generate tremendous publicity, and, for that reason alone, it would be an excellent move for my career.'

'But it's my hospital!' she cried. 'What about my career?'

His arms tightened and for a moment she thought he understood. Then she realised he was chuckling!

'It's not *your* hospital, in the sense that you own it, Meggie,' he assured her. 'It's a government hospital and must be held accountable. And you're not to blame for this rampant infection. The fellow bringing the action was probably infected before you went to Shorehaven. And if he's suffered, which he has, doesn't he deserve some compensation? The hospital has insurance to cover this kind of thing.'

'Insurance covers negligence,' she cried. 'You'd be proving negligence against the hospital.'

'You can't take it personally,' he argued, rubbing his hands up and down her arms in a soothing motion.

'Can't take it personally?' she repeated, pushing her shaking body away from him so that she could turn and glare into his face. 'And how else am I supposed to take it? Was this part of the getting-back-together thing? Was it because it would make it easier for you to take the case if you lived in Shorehaven? And I'm supposed to kiss you goodbye in the morning, and say,

Have a nice day in court, dear, then go off and be interrogated and humiliated by you later—and not take it personally!'

He reached out and held her by the shoulders, his face soft with understanding, but his eyes not giving an inch.

'Both our jobs will cause hardship for the other at times. It's what we must adjust to.' He gave her a little shake. 'Do you think I enjoy your getting out of bed in the middle of the night when you're called to the hospital, or phoning friends to break an arrangement when you're unavoidably delayed?'

'That's different,' she muttered. 'I have no choice but to go when I'm needed, or to stay if an operation isn't completed.'

'And you think I have easier choices? Can I say to someone who needs me to fight their case, No, I can't do it because it might hurt my wife's sensibilities? Does that person deserve to have a less qualified barrister fight for them any more than your patient deserves to have a less qualified doctor perform his operation?'

Had he practised this conversation? she wondered as she tried to find words to match his reasoned, rational argument. How could she explain how she had felt in court; or how much of her hard-won confidence was tied up in her job? And should she have to explain? Surely if he loved her as he said he did, he should know and understand this?

The thoughts raced through her head, immobilising her brain, so it surprised her to realise he was speaking again, explaining things—placatory, appeasing, solidly reasonable things.

'. . .so much for trust. . .didn't say which side. . . consider Gemma, too!' Random phrases tugging in her mind. Then something clicked and she looked at him in blank horror.

He couldn't mean. . .! Couldn't think. . .! Not Gemma! Not her precious child!

She struggled to her feet and fled, nausea racking her body.

'You stay away from Gemma!' she shouted. 'And stay away from me! You with your rational, reasoned arguments, and your theorising. You used to talk about putting myself into your skin, telling me I should see things from your point of view! What about my point of view?'

The last words were a sobbing cry of despair, flung over her shoulder as she raced to the top of the rock slab.

'Meg, wait!' he called after her. 'Don't be stupid. You can't climb down in such a state. Don't try it without the rope.'

'Better dead than tied to you.' Her fury flung the words at him, but she turned and climbed down cautiously. He would have to coil the rope, gather up the pitons and slings, and heft the backpack onto his back. And she had always been a better climber, using skill to outmatch his strength.

Her feet found tiny toe-holds, her fingers clung, then moved and clung again. As careful as a cat, she made her way down, swiftly and surely, the tightening anger helping, not hindering, her movements. At the rock ledge beneath the slab she turned aside, taking a track they never used down towards a more frequented picnic area. Now she slipped and stumbled down through the peaceful bush, desperate to reach the bottom of the mountain—to get away.

'Help!'

At first she thought it was a bird cry, the word so weak and indistinct that it floated past her ears, but the second time she recognised the sound and even heard the desperation.

It came from her right, and she edged off the path, heading towards a narrow ledge above the steep northern slopes of the mountain.

'Where are you?' she called, then heard Jonathon's voice blot out any answer. 'Be quiet, Jonathon!' she yelled. 'There's someone needing help.'

She called again.

'We're on the cliff face!' the voice responded, a young woman or a youth by the sound of it.

'Stay where you are until I reach you, Meg,' Jonathon ordered. 'I can see you through the trees.'

'I'll go as far as the ledge, but won't walk out on it,' she promised, knowing they must work together if they were to have any hope of rescuing the trapped climbers.

She edged her way through the bush until she reached the place where the cliff reared above her.

'Where are you?' she called again.

'We're down here, below the big bluff. My friend fell; he's broken his leg and is lapsing into unconsciousness now and then. We've been here all night.'

Meg's heart thudded into overdrive. Both would be suffering from exposure, and the friend could have other injuries besides his broken leg.

She lay on the ledge and inched forward, peering down towards the voice. About thirty feet below, and further to the right, she could see a large pair of grubby sneakers pointing upwards to the sky. There was another ledge there, she remembered, below a chimney that looked as if it would provide an easy way to the top.

A rustling in the bushes behind her indicated Jonathon's arrival; then she felt his hands grasp her ankles and haul her back onto safer ground. He helped her stand up and for a moment his hands lingered on her skin.

'Did they try the chimney?' he asked, turning away to hammer a piton into a rock crevice on the bluff.

'I'd say so,' she muttered, embarrassed now by her earlier outburst, but still jittery with anger. 'The leader must have slipped and fallen, crashing back onto the lower ledge. He's hurt, Jonathon. I'll have to go down and see what I can do.'

'All you can do in the circumstances is basic first aid, Meg, and I can do that as well as you can.' His green eyes dared her to argue.

'But I'm lighter,' she pointed out with irrefutable logic. 'You can anchor me far more effectively than I can anchor you.'

His lips tightened and his face grew pale but he slipped a harness around her waist and clipped two ropes to it.

'Is there room on the ledge for another person?' he called down.

'I suppose so,' the voice said doubtfully.

'I'll come back up if there's nothing I can do,' Meg said quickly as Jonathon's lips moved in a silent curse. 'One of us will have to go for help to get the injured man off the ledge. We could never pull him up safely.'

He reached for her again and his hands bit into her shoulders but all he said was, 'Look at the chance of lowering him to the base of the mountain, Meg, and be careful.'

His fingers gripped momentarily, then he was handing her the extra equipment and issuing orders with the sharpness of a staff sergeant.

'Hit at least two of these into the rock face above the ledge when you get there. There are lengths of short rope in the backpack. Fasten yourself to the ledge before you do anything and stay fastened, whatever happens,' he commanded. 'I'll use the free rope to send the pack down when you're organised. There's a basic first-aid kit and the blanket in it. If anyone comes up the track, I'll send them for help, but otherwise I'll have to go back down to the car and use my mobile phone.'

Meg nodded. 'We might be able to get the uninjured person up before you go,' she suggested. 'If so, there's a Thermos of tea and some sandwiches in my bag on the back seat.'

It was Jonathon's turn to nod; then he leant forward and kissed her on the lips, a firm pledge that stilled her heartbeats.

'Keep talking to me as you go!' he ordered as she edged herself along the ledge, her back to the drop below her. She watched him wedge himself in position on the slope, the two ropes looped around his waist. His strong hands played them out towards her, and she imagined she could feel his tension transmitting itself along the nylon fibres.

'I'll be all right,' she whispered, then forced her mind away from Jonathon and concentrated on the task ahead of her.

If she remembered correctly there were good hand- and toe-holds in the cliff face once she was around the protruding lip of stone that cut her ledge off from the chimney. It was the same overhang that made the chimney dangerous, because climbers had no way of getting around it.

'I'm at the overhang,' she told Jonathon. 'I've got a good belay and will drop off this ledge here and swing across into the chimney lower down. Can you hold me?'

'Can you trust me?' he asked in a rough, dry voice, then he added warningly, 'Don't push out too hard with your feet!'

His voice sounded very 'English,' as if tension had tightened all his vowels. She thought about his question for a moment. Yes, she would trust him with her life— then why not with their future?

'Are you ready to swing?' he called, and she banished the distractions.

'Going now!' she yelled.

I must be stupid, she thought as she launched herself into space. I haven't climbed for four years, and here I am, swinging out over a precipice on a thin nylon rope.

Her feet hit the rock face and scrabbled for a moment before finding slight protrusions to take her weight. She let go of the rope with one hand, and reached for the cliff, finding a good finger grip almost immediately.

'I'm back on the rock,' she called, hoping she didn't sound as breathless as she felt.

'I can see you now,' the voice cried from below. 'If you go a bit further to your left you'll find the chimney. It's easy from there down to here.'

Meg inched her way towards the chimney, reporting to Jonathon once she'd squashed herself into the narrow defile and could rest her aching legs and arms. She hammered in another piton to make the way back up secure, slipped the rope through the sling and clambered down to the lower ledge.

The young woman greeted her with a tremulous hug, tears of relief streaming down her cheeks. Meg took one look at her pale face and shaking hands, and wondered if the girl would be able to climb back up along the rope trail. She would have to! There was standing room only on the ledge, and if she was to make the injured man comfortable she would need all the available space.

'I'm a doctor,' she said quietly. 'I'll do what I can for your friend, and Jonathon, the fellow at the top, will organise a rescue party, but first I need to get you up there out of the way.'

The girl, who introduced herself as Nan, nodded. Meg saw that she had roped herself and her friend, now introduced as Trevor, to the cliff. If she was sensible enough to do that, she should be able to manage the climb with Jonathon acting as anchor and taking some of her weight.

Meg drove in another piton and clipped her harness to it, then yelled up to Jonathon to send down the pack. When it came slithering down on the free-falling rope Meg grabbed it, and secured it to the cliff with another clip. She unzipped the top and produced a fruit bar.

'Now,' she turned to Nan, 'you eat this while I secure you to the ropes.' She unwrapped the bar as she spoke and thrust it into the girl's hands. Orders sometimes worked better than requests! She removed the first clip from her waist and fastened it to the girl's rope, swapping it for the clip that harnessed the girl to the cliff. Then she clipped the free rope to the back of the girl and patted her on the shoulder.

'I want you to climb back up the way I came down. Jonathon will anchor you if you slip and fall and will have the second rope to haul you up if necessary, but he wants to go for help as soon as possible, so if you can make it up on your own you will save precious time.'

Meg watched as Nan's anxious eyes glanced down at her immobile friend, then she saw the girl tense, making a visible effort to pull herself together. She munched obediently at the bar, wiped her hands on the seat of her shorts, and began to test the ropes.

'You've done well to get him through the night,' Meg told her, not wanting to ask questions in case the memories destroyed the composure the girl was fighting to regain. 'But now the most important thing is to get help. Jonathon won't leave the top until you're up there, so you'll have to go. As soon as you're out of the way I'll examine your friend and let you know what's happening, OK?'

'He'll be all right, won't he?' Nan whispered.

'I'm sure he will,' Meg told her, then called to let Jonathon know the ascent was beginning. 'Off you go,' she said. 'Yell out if you need a rest and don't be afraid to let Jonathon take your weight. When you get to the overhang, swing to the right. There are two pitons holding the rope and you've the second rope as an extra precaution. Once you've swung around the bluff, you're on another ledge and it's an easy scramble.'

Nan tried a wavery smile then set off, clambering up the face above Meg to leave her room to move across and examine the patient.

'Nan's on her way,' she called upward to Jonathon, then she tested her weight against the new safety lines, and crawled along the ledge towards the young man.

He was conscious, eyes open as he gazed unseeingly upward.

'You've got Nan away, then,' he mumbled, and Meg felt a surge of relief. If he was lucid enough to be following what was happening there was unlikely to be any brain damage. 'Bloody stupid thing to do, trying the chimney!' he muttered.

Meg felt his forehead, then slipped her fingers beneath his chin to feel for a pulse. The faint beat and the cold clamminess of his skin worried her, but there was little she could do apart from make him comfortable.

'Which leg have you hurt?' she asked and he waved his right hand. 'Rescuers will have to either lower you down or hoist you up,' she told him, peering over the ledge to see what lay below. 'Up means a helicopter, which is horribly expensive and can be dangerous for the flight crew working so close to the cliff face, but down could be more uncomfortable for you.'

'Down would be fine—don't worry about making it first-class travel,' he whispered and Meg smiled.

'Down might be possible,' she said, noticing how the cliff dropped away below them. From where she was she could see a cleared area at the foot of the mountain. She called her findings up to Jonathon, describing a rough track that seemed to lead from the clearing back towards the main picnic area.

'The emergency-rescue people will probably know the ledge,' he yelled back, then continued his encouragement of Nan, urging her upward as if she could make it by his will-power alone.

Meg pushed the backpack over her shoulder, clipped her harness to the rope that was slung around the young man's body, and edged along the rim of the ledge to reach a square-foot space of solid rock beyond his feet.

'I've got five bandages we carry in case of snake-bite,' she explained. 'I'm going to squat down here and bind your legs together so the good one can make a splint for the other.'

She manoeuvred the backpack round so that it hung in front of her and reached in for the elastic bandages Jonathon always carried. Pushing them into her shorts' pockets, she felt again, and pulled out the first-aid kit. She could use the rigid lid of the box to splint his knees and prevent their bending.

Once organised, she began, her hands moving cautiously as she tried to save the young man pain, and keep her own precarious balance.

'Nan's up and we're heading back to the car,' Jonathon called.

Relief washed over her. All she had to do was make the young man as comfortable as she could, and wait for the professionals to come and take over.

'Take care, Meg!' The words floated down, filled with a deep anxiety. Could he care so much about her safety yet not care about her 'life'?

She blinked away the distractions and concentrated on getting the legs bound together, tightly enough to hold the broken limb in place, but not enough to cut off circulation. Finishing the awkward task, she edged back along towards her patient's head and settled herself on the ledge, legs dangling into space.

'You OK?' she asked, and saw a wan smile stretch his pale lips. 'I'm going to shuffle along a bit and lift your head into my lap,' she explained. 'That way I can help you drink and pass you food more easily. Have you been taking painkillers?'

'Nan's been doling them out at regular intervals,' he replied. 'I can stand the pain; it's the not being able to move about that gets to me.'

'You start wriggling about and you'll save us the bother of a rescue party,' she warned him.

'Nan told me that!' he said and grinned again.

'She's pretty special, this Nan?' Meg teased, and saw the flush that coloured his white cheeks.

'She's wonderful,' he breathed. 'And like a damned idiot I got her into this impossible situation. She's sat there all night, where you're sitting, holding onto me and telling me we'd be all right. She's the bravest woman in the world! I hope she's OK.'

His voice quavered and Meg swallowed hastily, then brushed her fingertips across his forehead, soothing the pain of love.

'Jonathon will look after her,' she promised. 'Try to sleep; it will pass the time.'

The young man closed his eyes obediently, and Meg stared out over the treetops, her fingers stroking his skin while her mind wandered between the past and the present.

The young man's love was physically protective. He had wanted to take care of his Nan but had led her into danger. It seemed as though protecting the 'weaker sex' from physical harm was still instinctive in the male of the species, yet those instincts didn't stretch into the realms of the inner person. Jonathon saw her reaction as emotional rather than rational—and emotions didn't need protection!

She brooded over his potential involvement in a case against the hospital, labelling it egocentric, unfeeling—treacherous.

Or was she overreacting? Would he seriously consider taking such a case, or was he setting her up, waiting for her reaction so that they could debate the semantics of the rights to legal representation? Had she dropped into a trap he'd laid at her feet?

She shook her head. He was excited by the prospect of such a big case, already thinking about the positive benefits of the publicity.

She frowned at the eagle that swooped down the cliff face. Her body clamoured for the excitement and vitality Jonathon could provide, her mind longed for stimulating companionship—the challenging clash of his quick intelligence—but her heart remembered aching, and it whispered words of caution. There were still too many obstacles on the path ahead to go plummeting back into a relationship. And was he already involved in this case he'd mentioned so casually? Was that why he'd been visiting Gemma? Why he was hanging round the hospital?

She watched the eagle fall like a stone into the tops of the trees, intent on some tiny prey.

But didn't people who'd suffered because of MRSA deserve some compensation? Didn't Gemma?

The questions whispered sedulously in her mind and she shuddered. Of course people were entitled to some recompense, especially those who would suffer financial hardship as a result of their fight with the infection.

'Don't stop!' Trevor murmured, and she looked down to see that her fingers had dropped away from his face. 'It feels like love, that kind of touch—soft and gentle and comforting. Is your love like that?'

CHAPTER NINE

Soft and gentle and comforting? Maybe the ecstatic, uncomfortable, rapturous and agonising bliss she and Jonathon had shared had been something else. Deciding it was safer to ignore the question, Meg steered the conversation towards mountaineering, talking determinedly until she heard Jonathon calling to her from the ledge above them.

'The rescue crew should be here in about half an hour,' he told her. 'They know the ledge well and will climb up from the clearing rather than down from here. How's your patient?'

'He's as comfortable as I can make him,' she replied.

'Where's Nan?' Trevor whispered urgently, and Meg repeated the question.

'She's down at the car. I drove across to the main picnic area. The rescue team will go through that way and pick her up.'

Meg felt the tension drain from the young man's shoulders.

'Trevor says thanks!' she called upward, then she smiled reassuringly at her patient. 'It won't be much longer now!'

But her own unease was less easily soothed. Jonathon's presence on the ledge above her was like a tangible cloud of doom hovering over her head. It was one thing to storm away from him on the mountain top and trust to providence she would get a lift back to civilisation, but not so easy to refuse to speak to him once the rescue was effected.

'Do you want to leave him for the experts and climb back up to here? It would give them more room to work on the ledge,' Jonathon asked as the rescue van pulled into the clearing below her.

Trevor grimaced anxiously at her, and she smiled again.

'I'll wait here,' she called. 'Once the crew gets up with longer ropes, I should be able to abseil down, and I might be able to make Trevor more comfortable for his trip to hospital.'

There was no reply and, for a moment, she wondered if he had left the ledge above them. Then she heard a vehicle and Jonathon's shout, and knew he would wait until the rescuers arrived. Would he then return to his car and drive away, knowing that someone would arrange for her to be driven back to town?

The rescue team worked with a speed and efficiency that only dedicated practice could achieve, and Meg found herself marvelling at their competence. Once a strong anchor point had been established above the ledge, a light stretcher was drawn up. Two men, dangling from the cliff face to maximise the space, lifted Trevor onto the stretcher and strapped him in before signalling to those below that his descent was about to begin.

Meg held her breath as the stretcher slipped from view, releasing it only when she heard Nan's glad cry echoing upwards.

'Your turn now,' the handsome young rescuer said. 'Are you experienced enough to abseil down on your own or would you like to do it in double harness?'

'I'll manage on my own,' she told him with a grin,

'as long as it's like riding a bicycle—once learnt, never forgotten!'

He smiled back at her and dug a pair of leather mittens out of a bulging pocket. 'Slip these on to protect your palms, then show me how you fix the ropes and hold your hands.'

'Not taking my word for my competence!' Meg mocked, and won another smile. She twisted the rope around her body, then turned so that he could secure a safety rope to the back of her harness.

'Take it slowly and don't forget to kick off from the wall when you reach the part where the cliff ducks away,' he warned, then he braced himself against the cliff to take her weight as she launched herself over the edge.

'Well done, Meggie! You're down now!'

Strong arms reached out to grab her legs, slipping up to waist, then shoulders. She dropped the rope and felt it pulled free, while a click told her the safety catch had been released. Jonathon turned her in his arms and drew her close against his body, and the thudding beat of his heart hammered against her ribs.

The feeling that she had come home at last was so strong that she wanted to stay wrapped in his arms forever, but the argument on the top of the mountain was too fresh in her mind for her to give in to a rash impulse. She disentangled herself carefully and, unable to meet his eyes, she turned away, crossing to where Nan hovered over Trevor.

'They're taking him to hospital in Brisbane,' the girl said, her eyes huge with anxiety.

'I'm sure you'll be allowed to travel with him,' Meg assured her. 'If necessary I'll say you need treatment for shock. It's probably true.' She grinned cheerfully, but Nan refused to be comforted.

'But the car. . .! Someone must drive his car back to Brisbane, to the hospital, in fact, if that's where we'll both end up. It's new—well, second-hand, but new to Trev. We were celebrating his buying it by coming up here to climb.'

'I'll drive it back to Brisbane for you, if Trevor agrees,' Meg suggested, aware that she was secretly relieved by this unexpected solution to her own problem.

Nan's eyes brimmed with tears, and Trevor mumbled his thanks, sleepy now the rescue team's painkilling injection was taking effect.

'Do you want me to meet you in Brisbane?'

Jonathon's voice jolted through her. He must have walked over to join them while she was comforting Nan.

'There's no need for that,' she said—too abruptly. 'I can get the bus back down to the coast. I won't want to leave the hospital until I know he's comfortable.'

'As you wish.' The cold tone of the words chilled her heart but she knew it was the way things had to be. She turned and watched him walk away, his shoulders square, head high, hands that had held her, teased and tantalised her, swinging easily by his side.

Did practice make walking away easier? she wondered sadly, then she turned her attention to the two young people who still believed in the all-conquering power of love.

By seven o'clock next morning, Meg was glad to get out of the flat, where unanswerable questions bounced at her from the walls, and memories taunted her resolution.

Returning to work was like coming out of a dark tunnel, but although the hospital world was light and bright and familiar she sensed the lack of warmth in it. Could she ever go back within the clear professional guidelines she had drawn up for herself years ago, or had Jonathon's reappearance broken down too many barriers? Did she need friendships and relationships within her work arena now?

She went straight to the ward, anxious to see Mrs Carseldine, the diabetic patient she was due to operate on later in the day. A dextrose drip had been ordered, and she had left instructions for the patient's serum glucose to be monitored regularly, as stress, or pre-operative anxiety, could alter glucose metabolism.

'They are looking after me so well,' Mrs Carseldine assured her. 'Lovely nurses—so kind! And they tell me I'll have my own room after the operation, although I'm only a public patient.'

Meg smiled at her chirpy enthusiasm.

'I can keep a closer eye on you in your own room,' she explained. 'Now, you're first on my list this morning. That is so the fasting necessary for the operation does not unbalance your levels any more than is absolutely necessary. A nurse will do a correlation of fingerstick glucose and urine sugar and acetone before you come up to Theatre, and you'll be given a pre-med that will make you sleepy.'

Mrs Carseldine nodded, her eyes bright as she followed Meg's explanations.

'Because of the diabetes, you are more susceptible to infection after the operation, and the best way to pick that up is through a change in your glucose control. We also believe that, if we can keep your glucose level balanced, we can help prevent infection.'

And what if the staph isn't out of the hospital? she wondered, knowing that this particular patient was more at risk. Could she survive the onslaught of a bacterium as virulent as MRSA?

And, if she didn't, wouldn't her family deserve some recompense for the mother who money could never replace? an imp whispered in her ear.

Ignoring the imp, she spoke again to her patient, explaining that diabetic meals had been ordered, but that Kate Allen would be in to see her some time after the operation, to check if there was anything special she required, or to suggest treats that might tempt her to eat when she wasn't feeling up to food.

'I'll make certain I eat,' her patient assured her. 'I want to be out of this place as soon as possible. I've three kids at home who need a firm hand, even if it is raised from the bedroom.'

One of the men who had lost a leg following surgery and Golden Staph infection had five children, Meg remembered, but she forced the thought away.

'We'll want you to stay at least one night after the operation to keep IV fluids and antibiotics flowing into you, and to enable us to monitor your glucose levels. After that, providing there is no sign of trouble, you can go. As long as you're sensible when you get home,' she added in an admonitory tone.

'I've been sensible for twenty years,' Mrs Carseldine replied. 'I'm the best darn foot-examiner in the business, and I never miss a meal or fail to check my glucose levels. How else could I have had three successful pregnancies?'

Meg smiled her congratulations, and moved on, stopping to speak to other patients, and to bow to the remaining Japanese.

'Gemma's longing to see you if you've time to look in on her,' the sister on duty told her. 'She stayed last night at Mark's place and he dropped her off while you were with Mrs Carseldine. I gather she's had a super time.'

The thought of seeing Gemma lifted her spirits—momentarily! Yet, as she hurried towards the room, thoughts of staph and compensation still niggled in the back of her mind and she wondered about the validity of the righteous indignation she had hurled at Jonathon.

The little girl was flushed with excitement, still dressed in her 'going out' clothes, the pale blue skirt and blouse Meg had given her for her 'unbirthday'. Two months ago the staff had decided to give her a day to celebrate as her own and chosen the chaplain's birthday as the date. Meg remembered the excitement of that day, and a similar flush on the child's cheeks, although then it had been a flush of fever—then it had been the first sign that the staph infection was winning!

'Did you have a great time?' she asked, sitting on the edge of the bed and pushing back the fine fair hair.

Gemma needed no other prompting, launching into excited chatter about all the wonders she had seen, and all the marvellous things she had done.

'And I met a man who only had one leg, and he was walking just like Mark and all the other people. He had to lift up his trousers to show me because I didn't believe him! He said I'd be running around like all the other kids before I knew it!'

The wonder in Gemma's voice touched Meg. In the past, Gemma had shown fear and trepidation towards this next step in her rehabilitation, but now there were signs of eager anticipation.

'And Margaret said I could come and stay again next weekend, and that she would go with me to Brisbane for my fittings.'

Excitement bubbled through the words, though it took Meg a moment to remember that Mark's wife was called Margaret. And hadn't she been working? Could she afford the time to take Gemma to Brisbane?

She nodded, and murmured approval of the plans, needing to add little to keep the flow of information going, and filing away the bits she would check with Mark later.

'Do you know you're being shifted back closer to the other children today?' Meg asked, when the chatter ceased momentarily.

To her amazement, Gemma smiled and nodded, obviously happy about the move.

'It won't be for long,' she told Meg confidently. 'Especially since I'll go out at weekends.'

A tiny shaft of unease struck deep into Meg's heart. As Gemma, reminded by her own words of future treats, prattled on about Mark and Margaret, Meg forced herself to share the child's delight, banishing the feeling she now recognised as jealousy. She touched a finger to the smiling face and assured herself that she was pleased the young couple were taking such an interest in her special patient.

When she said goodbye and left she realised that Gemma was more than ready for the outside world. Had she kept her in the hospital longer than necessary? And had her own loneliness and attachment to the child contributed to that decision?

The thought depressed her, but the one that followed was even worse! If she had been wrong about that, could she be wrong about other things?

'There's a message to say the boss wants to see us.'
Bill's voice broke into her reverie. He was waiting in
the corridor outside Gemma's room. 'Do you want to
prolong the agony by doing a ward-round first?'

'Trouble?' she asked.

'Isn't it always?' he said, then grinned at her. 'Maybe
he enjoys the stimulation of clashing with you. It might
start his week in high good humour.'

She sighed. Her future depended on James Clarke's
approval and support and she hated being at odds with
him. If only they could agree on the MRSA business!

'We'd better go now,' she said with a bleak sigh
of resignation. 'Mrs Carseldine's op is scheduled for
nine-thirty and, besides, bad news doesn't improve
with keeping.'

They took the lift to the top floor and walked
towards the chief superintendent's office.

'If it's about vancomycin again, I've read up on some
more information that will support your theory,' Bill
murmured. 'Some obscure college in the United States
has done a survey on its prophylactic use and found
its effectiveness can't be proved. We could show him
the figures—'

Meg was smiling her delight at this news when the
door opened.

'Oh, there you are,' James greeted them. 'I was
about to give up on you and take Mr Prior down to
Obstetrics.'

Meg felt her face stiffen, and her heart accelerate.
She heard Bill acknowledging an introduction, then
Jonathon's voice protesting at the use of his surname,
and James explaining something about insurance companies, advice, safeguards.

'But sit down, both of you,' James said genially,

drawing them into the room and waving them into comfortable chairs. Meg felt her legs give way of their own accord and she slumped down into a chair.

He wasn't ambulance chasing, or drumming up business for a case against the hospital. Trust! That was all he'd asked of her or wanted from her. The trust he'd lost when his father had confessed to a mammoth, life-long lie.

She looked up into his face, but no emotion showed; certainly none of the bleak emptiness she felt within herself.

'Jonathon is looking at the overall functioning of the hospital, at the procedures and safeguards we have in place at the moment. Once he has a good idea of how we run, he will go back to our insurance company, and, using their records of past claims worldwide, advise if there are extra precautions we should take, or new measures we should put in place, to protect ourselves from claims of negligence.'

James smiled cheerfully at them as he finished his little speech, and Meg realised he had given it before. If other staff knew about this investigation, why hadn't she heard that such a person was in the hospital? And why hadn't Jonathon told her the real reason he was 'hanging around' instead of letting her believe. . .?

He was replying to a question from Bill, but all she could hear was one word; trust. It seemed to be written in neon letters in her head, flicking on and off with an infuriating persistence, while its single syllable drummed in her ears.

'This is a new service offered by the insurance company,' Jonathon explained, 'so I'll be learning as I go along. For the first few days I wandered around the place, trying to get a feel for what was happening.

Now that I'm no longer incognito, so to speak, I'm hoping that all the staff and consultants will be willing to talk to me. I believe they have the knowledge and expertise to point out any areas where improvements might be made, or tell me ideas they would like to try in order to provide added safeguards for the patients.'

Meg heard his emphasis on the final word and wondered if he'd done it deliberately, to distance himself from James's contention that it was 'the hospital' and 'the staff'—such impersonal entities!—that needed protection.

She glanced up to see Jonathon watching her intently, and felt a surge of heat rise from her toes.

I'm on your side, he seemed to be saying. You've always said the patients' well-being must be the first consideration.

'We'll be happy to cooperate,' she said stiffly. 'The theatre staff will show you around any time, and you're welcome to stand in on any operation. I presume you'll have to do that to get some idea of how the theatres work.'

He nodded gravely. 'That's one of the reasons I asked to see you first. I believe the orthopaedic specialists have lists today and I would like to begin with the theatres for obvious reasons.'

Meg heard the unspoken dread of 'Staph' echo round the room, and bowed her head in acquiescence. She tried to think of something to say, but the accusations she had flung at Jonathon only yesterday blotted out all thought and her body battled with its own memories.

'Meg and I usually use Theatres Two and Three on operating days, while outside consultants use Four. Five is kept for general surgery and One for emergency use.' Bill came to her rescue with his matter-of-fact explanation. 'We start at nine-thirty and go between the two theatres, so we are working in one while the other is being cleaned down for the next op.'

'Then I'll see you in Theatre at nine-thirty.'

How could he sound so relaxed? Meg wondered as Bill ushered her out of the office. How could he sit there and act as if nothing had happened?

'Were you ever married to him?' Bill's question jolted her out of her abstraction.

'Of course not,' she said crossly. 'And the sooner that stupid story is killed by some more interesting gossip, the better.'

'I only asked,' he protested mildly, stepping aside to allow her to enter the lift, 'because you did seem to go to pieces back there. As if his being in the same room had thrown you off balance.'

'Well, it didn't and I'm not!' she snapped, then realised that neither protest made much sense. 'What we have to do is forget about Jonathon Prior and concentrate on our work. There's nothing James Clarke would love more than to find we were negligent in some aspect of our procedures. Then he could blame us for the staph infections and exonerate his precious hospital!'

'But Prior's not here to look into the staph business,' Bill protested.

'Oh, no?' Meg muttered, still smarting from her own embarrassment and confusion. 'You just be certain that you don't miss a step in anything you do today— particularly in checking the disposal of used material and the sterilisation of instruments. Remember all the points the infection-control committee made at its last meeting and make sure we're following them.'

She saw Bill's frown, but the lift doors opened

at that moment and she swung away from him, walking briskly down the corridor to escape further probing.

They were gowning up when Jonathon walked in, seeming as relaxed in this environment as he had been in court. One of the sisters hurried to assist him into a gown, but Meg's fingers trembled on her ties until Bill swung her around to take over the fastening of her gown. Sensing her tension, he broke the straining silence.

'Will you run an insulin drip when you operate on Mrs Carseldine?'

Meg eased the air from her constricted lungs. 'I don't think so,' she replied, in what she hoped was a calm and competent voice. 'Releasing the contracture of her hand is a thirty-minute procedure and normally would be done in day surgery. She should be covered by the half-dose of insulin until we get her back to the ward, and after that we can administer it as needed.'

'Isn't a Dupuytren's contracture rare in a woman of her age?' Bill persisted, and Meg decided to play along with him. It was better than listening to her own erratic heartbeats.

'Very rare. It could be genetic in her case, as she vaguely remembers her grandfather having a "claw hand". It's twice as common in men as in women, and usually only found in people of European origin. Mrs Carseldine's family came from Germany, so that fits.'

'But it's age-related as well, isn't it?'

Why on earth is he going on about this? Meg wondered, then looked up to see a frown darkening his usually cheerful face. He's concerned for me, she realised. Concerned about my behaviour, about my reactions to Jonathon. And probably wondering whether that will affect my ability to operate efficiently. That's why he's got us prattling on like a couple of medical textbooks!

'Isn't it?' Bill repeated, dragging Meg's attention back to his chosen topic.

'Generally more common with age, and with other conditions like epilepsy and alcoholism,' she agreed, pulling a cap down over her hair. 'But, like Alzheimer's, when a younger person suffers it progresses much more quickly. Now, let's go or we'll never get through the day.'

She led the men through into the theatre, greeted Brian and the other members of the surgical team and introduced Jonathon as an 'observer'. Had the nursing staff been told why he was here?

She shrugged the thought aside. She could hardly ask them to be extra-careful in front of him—and maybe it was best they didn't know. At least that way he'd see how well they always performed their tasks!

Somehow she worked through the day, her hands performing their skilled movements with a mechanical efficiency. Jonathon's presence in the room set every nerve tingling, and, when his green gaze met hers, by accident on her part, she shivered at the shadows she saw reflected there. But what could she say or do to chase them away? And were they her responsibility?

He left the theatre as they finished the last patient, and an audible sigh echoed round the table.

'Been a bit like having a ghost at Christmas dinner,' Bill remarked as they finished up for the day.

'The morgue'd be more cheerful than this place today,' Brian replied. 'And to think I used to like working with you two!'

'He's only doing his job,' Meg protested. 'It's in

our interests to let him see how we work.'

'Ours or the insurance company's?' Brian asked.
'And you're only defending him because you used to
be married to him.'

It was the final straw after a day of unbelievable
tension.

'I was not married to him!' Meg yelled. 'Not married
to him now—nor ever married to him, do you
understand?'

The theatre staff all stopped what they were doing
to gape at her, stilled into a macabre tableau of astonishment.

'OK, OK, you don't have to wake the patient!' Brian
grumbled. 'But the whole hospital's abuzz with it, so
the rumour must have started somewhere.'

I'll kill him, she thought, gritting her teeth so tightly
that they ached. He talks about trust! Even said he
still loved me! Yet he's started this rumour when he
knows how hospitals love a bit of gossip!

'This place might run a lot better if people spent
more time working and less talking about other
people's affairs,' she said bitterly. 'Maybe someone
might like to pass that on to him as one of the things
likely to improve services to patients.'

She strode away from their startled silence, stripping
off her theatre garb as she went. I don't care, she
assured herself over and over and over again, but deep
in her heart wounds had opened wider.

It was inevitable that he would be the only passenger
in the lift as she headed down towards the ward and
her small office.

'I was never married to you!' she raged, clenching
her hands into fists by her side and pouring out her
pain in anger.

He stood very still, looking at her with an intentness that both frightened and confused her.

'At the time you said our commitment was as real as any marriage, Meg,' he reminded her. 'To me it was,' he added simply.

The lift doors slid open and he stepped out, leaving her alone in the metal cage.

They *had* made a commitment, and, at the time, had believed it to be as binding as any marriage. Yet recently she had denied it, not once but many times. The thought made her feel sicker.

And now, when he'd returned and it had seemed that happiness was once more within her grasp, she'd refused the trust he'd asked for!

It was for the best, she told herself as she followed him out of the lift and scurried along the corridor, seeking the solitude of her office. There were too many obstacles for a relationship between them to ever work again—too many differences in the way they thought and felt and acted.

She sank down behind her desk and rested her head in her hands, knowing she must clear her mind of personal issues and concentrate on the rest of the day's work. But her body, which had been so conscious of his presence all day, ached now with loss, filled with a regret so deep that she knew the pain would never go away.

CHAPTER TEN

DURING the following fortnight Jonathon became a familiar figure around the hospital, but Meg managed to avoid meeting him face to face. Or was he avoiding her?

Whichever way it happened, she was glad, she told herself as she sat at her desk before Theatre one morning, but the jittery nervous tension that accompanied her through each day made a mockery of that contention. The sooner he was out of 'her' domain and she could concentrate fully on her work, the better.

The jangling summons of the phone interrupted her thoughts.

'Megan Groves,' she said automatically, signing a note while she waited for the caller to respond.

'It's Jonathon, Meg.'

Heartbeats stopped, then started into rioting arrhythmia.

'I wondered if I could do another day in theatre with your team today.'

Why? she wanted to ask. Why with my team? Anxiety killed the desire his voice had ignited.

'It's purely routine,' he added calmly, raising her anxiety to panic-level. Had he seen signs of negligence? Was he really here investigating the staph outbreak and using the insurance story as a cover?

'I suppose it's all right,' she stammered, while her mind raced through worse and worse scenarios. Could her team have been responsible? Could she have been responsible for Gemma's pain?

'Of course it's all right, Meg!' he said crossly, as if he could sense the despair she was experiencing. 'Although how I can convince you of that without trust, I don't know!'

The final words were rough, gruff and barely heard, but the click told her he'd disconnected before she could protest, or question him.

She closed her eyes for a moment, breathing deeply to regain control, then thought of the day's programme. The scheduled operations were routine—a hip replacement, followed by an arthroscopic examination of a knee, and the resetting of a badly broken arm. That could be tricky and she pulled out the file and went over the details of the original injury and treatment.

Reaching for the phone again, she dialled the theatre and asked for the special screws she would need to be collected from stock, then decided she would go up and check the supplies herself. The final operation for the day was a shoulder—an operation that would be good experience for Bill.

With her mind fixed firmly on the day's work and the instruments and prosthesis she would need, she stepped into the lift, and, too late, became aware of the only other passenger.

'We'll have to stop meeting this way,' Jonathon muttered, but the strained smile that accompanied the joke stole any ease it might have offered.

'When will you be finished here?' she asked, knowing she could not stand the tension his presence caused much longer.

'I finish up today,' he told her stiffly, and her

contrary body reacted with a clenching pain while her
mind filled with despair.

'Are you looking for the cause of the staph infections?' she whispered, desperately trying to make sense
of what was happening in both her private and professional worlds.

He frowned, and was about to say something when
the lift doors swung open.

'I've been looking for you, Meg,' Bill announced,
glancing at the controls to see that they were all heading for the fifth floor. 'I know you have me down for
the arthroscopy today, but I was wondering if I could
have a go at the rotator cuff as well.'

Meg smiled. It was a weak effort that grew stronger
when she saw a similar expression flicker across
Jonathon's lips. Even an animal as thick-skinned as an
elephant should have sensed the uneasiness in the lift,
yet Bill's enthusiasm for his work overrode all else,
and swept others along in its wake.

'It's all yours, but you'll have to be on your mettle.
Jonathon's standing in again,' she told him as they all
emerged in the foyer of the theatre floor.

'Great!' Bill responded, his glee undiminished by the
news that had spoilt her day. 'Want to see the best
team in the hospital at work once again?' he joked, and
strode off up the corridor with his white coat flapping
behind him.

They were a good team, Meg assured herself as she
followed reluctantly in his wake, her skin prickling with
awareness as Jonathon trod a mere half-pace behind
her. She ran through the list again in her mind and
pushed into the theatre determined to recapture her
enthusiasm for her work and the drive she needed as
she strove for perfection.

'Meg!' The low, deep murmur brought her spinning around, but whatever Jonathon was about to say was lost as they stared at each other, caught once again in a moment of instinctive recognition.

'Meg, which drill were you planning to use on the shoulder?' Bill's voice had a hollow ring to it, echoing out of the empty theatre.

She drew a ragged breath and turned away. The knowledge that she still loved Jonathon hammered in her heart, but she knew it was no good to hope for new beginnings. He had held out his hand—and his heart!—to her again and all he had asked for in return was trust. But she had been unable to crack open the shell she had built around her emotions, unable to risk the pain again—so she had hurt him instead, denying him the one thing he wanted from her.

She crossed the room to join Bill and lost herself in preparations for the day ahead. As the others entered she felt herself drawn into the strange unity of the operating-room and relished the feeling of completeness it gave her. They swung into action, and Meg forgot her fears about Jonathon's presence even if she was unable to forget the man himself.

'Well, here's your torn rotator cuff,' she told Bill as the last patient was wheeled in.

He turned from the panel where the X-rays were lit as guides to surgery, and grinned at her. 'Thank you, ma'am!' he said, snapping her a mock-salute. 'And will you condescend to assist?'

She bowed in reply and forced a smile. Poor Bill had had a trying day in his role as theatre jester, Jonathon's presence making all the team more wary and concerned.

'It will be an honour,' she insisted, then added a

warning. 'It's a complete tear, and, although the way you cut is optional, I always make the skin incision across the shoulder, then cut longitudinally through the muscle. I find the external wound heals better that way.'

Bill stepped into her position at the head of the table and she shifted easily to the assistant's spot. Two student nurses were present in the theatre, so she quietly explained about the supraspinatus tendon.

'It has a poor blood supply, so is weakened with ageing. Severe pain in the shoulder region and a lack of abduction in the arm is usually a sign of either a partial or complete tear of the rotator cuff of which the tendon is part. The object of this operation is to rejoin the tendon, and, in order to give it more room and prevent the stitched part rubbing against the bone and wearing thin again, we will remove some of the acromion.'

Both the nurses looked blank, and Meg had to smile, remembering how the sheer number of the names they had to remember—of bones, nerves, blood vessels and muscles—had daunted her during her student days.

'It's a bony extension at the top of the scapula or shoulder blade,' she explained. 'The tendons run through a narrow gap between its junction with the clavicle and the head of the humerus. When you get out of here, have a look at this area—' she wiggled her shoulder '—on your teaching skeleton, and you'll be able to see it clearly.'

While she spoke she watched Bill, and fitted her hands to the tasks he asked of her, using hooks to hold apart the muscle so that he could get into the narrow space and work efficiently.

'Now he's going to remove part of the bone,' she

said. 'The operation will be written on your schedule
as "Tendon Repair and Acromioplasty". The "-plasty"
is tacked onto any cosmetic surgery, and, although we
aren't doing this to make the patient look prettier, it
is still considered an elective surgical procedure.'

She felt rather than saw Bill's startled gaze flick to
her face and back to the wound. At the head of the
table, Brian stirred and she saw his eyes twinkling
above his mask. Was her light remark so unexpected
that they would both register it? she wondered, then
shivered as if the earth had moved beneath her feet.

For a few moments she had forgotten her doubts
about Jonathon's purpose in the theatre, forgotten it
enough to be making her own attempts at light-hearted
banter!

Bill was closing the wound when the message came
that she was needed in the ward. She slipped away
from the group around the table and stripped off her
gear. Much as she welcomed the chance to escape the
theatre before Jonathon could leave, concern over the
message nagged at her.

'His blood pressure's rising and he's running a high
temperature, but the wound doesn't look infected,'
Janet greeted her, leading Meg towards the bed of a
patient she had operated on two days earlier.

'Here's Doctor now,' she said cheerfully to Mr
Hawkins, then she bustled away, leaving Meg gazing
down at the obviously unwell patient.

'Do you feel sick? Nauseous?' she asked, picking up
the chart and noticing the rising temperature—in spite
of a continual drip of post-operational antibiotics.

'Not too bad,' her patient replied, 'but my head and
neck are aching something awful.'

Not a usual symptom for someone who'd had an

open reduction of a broken tibia and fibula, Meg thought grimly.

She bent over his leg, cradled by a half-plaster, but no tell-tale redness surrounded the neatly stitched wound.

'I'll do a culture and test for infection,' she told him. 'That should tell us what kind of bug has got hold of you, and how to treat it.'

'Whatever you say is OK by me,' Mr Hawkins told her, his eyes closing as he fought off the lethargy of pain and medication.

Janet returned with a tray of instruments, and held it while Meg took a small sample of the colourless seepage from the leg wound.

'Send it straight to the lab,' Meg told her, refusing to utter the fear that was in both their minds. 'If it's staph the culture will show.'

As she took Mr Hawkins' blood pressure and temperature, confirming the findings of the nurses, her mind argued the pros and cons of starting vancomycin immediately. It was such a toxic drug that she was reluctant to use it except against MRSA.

'I'll be back shortly,' she told Mr Hawkins, and walked slowly back to her office, where she pulled out her pharmacology book and opened it at anti-infectives.

What could it be, apart from MRSA, that the precautionary antibiotics she was using wouldn't control? The headache could be a symptom of any infection, but the neck pain?

She closed her eyes and visualised the patient lying in bed, his hand rubbing at his temple, and his jaw. His jaw! It had been his jaw, not his neck, that he'd been rubbing.

She searched through the indications listed for the drugs she'd given then looked up, and, in a superstitious relapse to childhood, crossed her fingers.

Heading back towards the ward, she met Bill. The gravity of his expression told her Janet had already spoken to him about Mr Hawkins.

'It might be OK,' she told him. 'I think it could be tooth trouble.'

He followed her back to the patient's bedside and watched as she bent and touched him gently on the shoulder.

'Show me again where it hurts,' she said, then smiled as he lifted his hand to cup his jaw then draw his fingers down his neck.

'It may be a tooth problem—an abscess—that's flared up coincidentally,' she told him. 'Would you mind if I looked in your mouth?'

'Turning dentist now?' Bill joked, but he leant forward to peer over her shoulder as she shone her small torch into their patient's mouth.

'It's hard to tell, but if it's an abscess it won't be obvious,' she murmured, feeling a little lost in the unfamiliar discipline. 'Could you try pressing your tongue against the teeth on that side, to see if any of them feel tender?'

They watched him close his mouth then saw the flinch as his tongue found the tender tooth immediately.

'I was feeling so bad that I didn't think of it being anything but my leg,' he said. 'What can I do about it?'

Meg smiled her relief. I'll change your antibiotics to something that should knock the abscess out as well as prevent infection in your leg. And, if you like, I'll get the hospital dentist to visit you. At least he'll be able to tell you if you need immediate treatment for it.'

Mr Hawkins smiled and thanked them, and Meg left Bill to finish the ward-round while she spoke to Janet about the drug changes.

'You want to check the post-ops?' Janet asked when they had finished with Mr Hawkins.

'Bill's doing them, but I've got a pile of office work to get through, so I'll wait for Mr Campbell to come down. He had the rotator-cuff repair and will probably be a few hours in Post-Op while they try to stabilise the pain.'

Janet grimaced, knowing the pain shoulder-operation patients invariably suffered. 'Well, get back to your office and I'll let you know when he comes down.'

Meg nodded and moved away, then realised she hadn't thought of Jonathon for an hour.

It was less than a month ago since she was congratulating herself on not thinking of him for weeks, she remembered sadly. She dropped down into her chair and began on the paperwork that dogged most of her spare time.

'Do you ever go home?'

Her head jerked up.

The subject of her thoughts was lounging against the doorjamb, his hands in his pockets, negligently at ease.

'I'm waiting for that last patient to come down from Post-Op,' she said carefully. 'Do you have to wait as well? Is that part of your duty to the insurance company?' Her voice was tight with the effort it took to keep it from trembling.

'Not tonight!' he said, a smile easing the tension on his face. 'I'm finished here—for a while, at least.'

'And what about the staph case you mentioned?'

she asked, not able to let go of her doubts.

'From all the rumours one hears, it's still being considered, but I doubt they'd find any evidence of
negligence.' He paused and she waited, staring up into
his unsmiling face. 'I've looked and not found any,'
he added, 'although I think there might be a couple
of areas where the system could be changed to provide
greater safeguards.'

'Such as?' she demanded, annoyed by his nonchalant
attitude.

He grinned, and her heart flipped over. He's not
grinning at you, she told it crossly, but her body had
long ceased to obey her mind where this man was
concerned.

'That's for me to know and you to find out,' he
teased, then the smile faded and he walked into the
room, dropping down into the chair opposite her.
'Actually, I have to go back and study the insurance
files before I can make any constructive suggestions.
At the moment, I have the glimmering of an idea, but
it may prove unnecessary or unworkable. You'll have
to wait and see the final report, unless. . .'

'Unless?' she echoed.

'Unless you'd like to have dinner with me.'

She stared at him across the desk, but his face
revealed nothing and his eyes were hidden behind
lowered eyelids and thick, tawny lashes.

'That wasn't what you were going to say,' she
accused, and saw the green flash as his eyelids flew up.
The green flash—and something that looked like pity?

'No, but I'll say that later—if you'll come.'

And how could she say no? Just having him in the
room with her brought a perverse and painful kind of
joy. When would she next be able to sit with him, to

hear his voice, and see his hands move as he talked; to watch his brow furrow when he thought and see the crinkly lines around his eyes and the deep crease in his cheek when he smiled?

'I have to wait for Mr Campbell to come down from Post-Op,' she said coolly, trying to hide the excitement she knew she shouldn't be feeling.

'I've asked Bill if he'd mind checking him for you,' he replied, and for a moment she wanted to yell at him again, to demand to know what right he had to do such a thing.

But she wanted to go so badly! Wanted to spend a little more time with him, alone, and in a semblance of peacefulness.

'I'll have to go home and change,' she objected, and saw him smile.

'I'll drive you. Any other excuses?'

She smiled herself—a tight-lipped little effort but better than nothing—and rang through to the ward to check with Bill before she left. While waiting for Janet to connect him she added, 'I'll have to see Gemma on my way out. They moved her back down to the children's ward.'

There was no reply, and she looked up to see a frown deepening on his face, but then Bill was talking and she switched her mind to work.

'I came by Gemma's room on my way up,' Jonathon told her as she replaced the receiver and pushed papers back into their folders and straightened her desk. 'The nurse on duty said she'd gone out.'

'Oh!' Disappointment stilled her hands for a moment, but then Jonathon was speaking again.

'Someone said the Mirabelle is a great restaurant. Should I make a booking?'

Meg frowned and nodded absentmindedly as her mind chased a false note somewhere in this conversation.

'I'll ring while you're changing,' he said cheerfully, standing up and waiting for her to precede him through the door.

She rose more slowly, still puzzled by an inconsistency she could not identify, but then he took her arm and the spinning vortex of her reaction to his touch sent all rational thoughts from her mind.

'Would you like a drink?' she asked when she had led him into her flat. Maybe a stiff gin might help her relax and behave normally, might still the pulsing waves of desire his attraction was generating.

'Not yet,' he responded. 'We might share a bottle of wine with our dinner. One glass will be enough for me; I'm driving, remember.' He looked around the room as if seeing it for the first time. 'You have a drink if you want one. I'm happy to sit for a while.'

Now that the opportunity was handed to her, Meg realised that a drink was not going to help. In fact, the way she felt, it might prove disastrous!

'I'll wait and join you in a glass of wine,' she said ungraciously. 'I won't be long.'

She hurried through to the bathroom and stripped off her clothes. Would cold showers work for women? she wondered, seeking to ease the torment of her passion for this man whose love she had rejected—whose trust she had betrayed.

'You look great,' he murmured when she finally appeared, but there was a gravity in his voice that frightened her. This wasn't the Jonathon who'd come back seeking a reconciliation, the Jonathon who'd offered her another chance. This was a stranger—holding her at arm's length with both his coolness and his careful conversation.

He led her out to the car, offering more snippets of information about his work. It wasn't until they pulled into the carpark of the classy restaurant, built out over the river, that she realised he was as uneasy as she was. At first she'd been glad of his chatter because it masked her own silence, but its constancy and repetition now worried her. Was he using all this talk to stop her asking questions, or to cover his own discomfort about what he had to say?

Once parked, he held open her car door, then took her arm to walk her through the marble-floored lobby of the hotel, past the huge urns of wild flowers and antique furniture, and into the restaurant that looked out over the dark, placid waters.

'Have you eaten here before?' he asked as the waitress departed to fetch a menu and wine list.

Do I go along with this polite conversation or demand to know what's bothering him? Meg wondered.

'No,' she told him, and was about to ask the question when the waitress reappeared.

Maybe he was right to wait, she decided, and asked about his father's health instead. He answered easily enough and she felt the constraints between them lessening, although her body kept up a constant clamouring for a smile, a touch, a hint of closeness.

They ate in silence, Meg pretending to appreciate the medley of tastes blended to tempt and delight them, and not knowing what he thought or felt about it all. When their plates were removed, and coffee ordered, Meg decided she could wait no longer.

'What's this all about, Jonathon?' she asked.

'It's about Gemma, Meg,' he said quietly, watching her across the table with an unnatural wariness.

'Gemma!' The reply stunned her. He'd asked her out to dinner to talk about Gemma! Disappointment flared through her, but dismay followed swiftly on its heels. 'You *were* here to spy!' she cried. 'You *are* going to sue!'

She flung her accusation venomously at him, and would have thrown the wine-glass as well if a waiter, sensing a disturbance, had not arrived to clear the table.

'Don't be stupid!' Jonathon growled as the man walked away. He reached out across the table and covered her clenched fists with his warm, strong hands. 'How many times do I have to tell you I'd never do anything to hurt you?'

Distracted by the silent messages bombarding her body, she drew back her hands and tried to concentrate on what he was saying.

'About Gemma,' he repeated. 'Not the staph infection but her future, Meg.'

Now the words penetrated the haze of longing and for a moment she was filled with a wild, ecstatic joy.

She raised her head to look at him, knowing her eyes must be brimming with hope, then dropped her gaze to the tablecloth when she read the concern and pity in his face.

'I thought. . .' she muttered.

'That maybe you could adopt her? That maybe she could be yours?' he prompted with a gentleness that brought tears to her eyes.

She nodded a mute reply.

'But did you, in your heart of hearts, believe it could

work that way?' he asked, and the gravity in his voice made her look up again.

His eyes shone with the love she had tried to pretend did not exist, the love he had kept so well hidden these last few tormenting weeks.

'I had no time to give a child,' she admitted. 'Especially one who needed the attention Gemma deserves. I knew that all along, but couldn't kill the dream.'

'Dreams are hard to kill,' he told her gruffly, 'unless there are new ones to take their place.'

There was a moment's silence, barely long enough to hear—or plant a tiny seed of hope!

'Your patient-welfare officer, Mark Reynolds, and his wife want to take Gemma, with a view to adopting her once the legal problems are ironed out.'

Mark and Margaret wanted to adopt Gemma? She thought she heard a sigh inside her, or was it a dream dying?

'Isn't that what you've wanted for Gemma, Meg? Don't you agree that she should go to people who will love and care for her forever, not be shifted from pillar to post like some rag doll?'

Of course I agree, she wanted to yell at him, but I wanted those 'people' to be me!

'How do you know about this?' she whispered.

He looked across the table at her, and she hated the pity and understanding that was evident in his eyes.

'Mark spoke to me about the legal implications when I first arrived at the hospital, then, once it was settled, he asked me to talk to you. He knows how much you love Gemma.'

Tears were burning behind her eyes, but they couldn't be for Gemma. Gemma was going to a caring, loving family. Gemma would be all right!

'So that's the only reason you asked me out to dinner? To tell me someone else was going to adopt Gemma?' To break my heart again? she added silently.

'Of course it wasn't,' he said crossly, reaching out and recapturing the hands that were pleating the edge of the tablecloth with a feverish urgency. 'I asked you out because I love you, you stupid woman! I've always loved you, and I always will, although heaven only knows why. You're the most prickly, defensive, irritating, infuriating, illogical female in the entire world!'

'You love me?' She blinked, as if the fog in her brain might be vanquished by clearer sight. 'After all I've done. . .the times I've let you down. . .my lack of trust? All of that, and you still love me?'

She frowned at him, and shook her head. She must be going mad. It was the shock of his sudden reappearance in her life, and all the strain of having him around and probably a hormonal imbalance caused by her irresponsible body!

'And you love me!' he added firmly. 'Although you sometimes have a strange way of showing it, and haven't yet sorted out your life sufficiently to admit it because you're still so damned focused on your future and frightened that love might deflect its course and throw you into chaos.'

'But—'

'No buts,' he admonished. 'We'll sort all that out later. Shall we go?'

'Go where?' she whispered, trying to make sense of what was happening. But love, or some chemical abnormality, had thrust rosy pink clouds into the space where her brain had once been.

'Go home!'

'Home?' she echoed with a misty smile, unable to

keep the hope and joy and rapture at bay any longer.

'Home,' he said firmly. 'Wherever you and I can be together, that will be our home.'

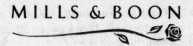

MILLS & BOON

MEDICAL ROMANCE

LOVE ON CALL

The books for enjoyment this month are:

BUSH DOCTOR'S BRIDE	Marion Lennox
FORGOTTEN PAIN	Josie Metcalfe
COUNTRY DOCTORS	Gill Sanderson
COURTING DR GROVES	Meredith Webber

Treats in store!

Watch next month for the following absorbing stories:

TENDER TOUCH	Caroline Anderson
LOVED AND LOST	Margaret Barker
THE SURGEON'S DECISION	Rebecca Lang
AN OLD-FASHIONED PRACTICE	Carol Wood

Available from W.H. Smith, John Menzies, Volume One,
Forbuoys, Martins, Woolworths, Tesco, Asda, Safeway and
other paperback stockists.

Readers in South Africa - write to:
IBS, Private Bag X3010, Randburg 2125.

Name that Song

How would you like to win a year's supply of simply irresistible romances? Well, you can and they're free! Simply solve the puzzle below and send your completed entry to us by 31st October 1996. The first five correct entries picked after the closing date will each win a years supply of Temptation novels (four books every month—worth over £100).

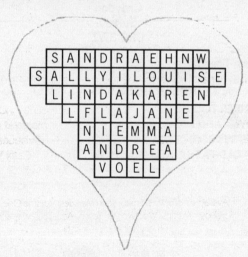

S	A	N	D	R	A	E	H	N	W
S	A	L	L	Y	I	L	O	U	I	S	E
L	I	N	D	A	K	A	R	E	N
L	F	L	A	J	A	N	E
N	I	E	M	M	A
A	N	D	R	E	A
V	O	E	L

Please turn over for details of how to enter ☞

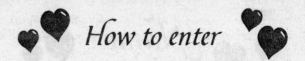 *How to enter*

To solve our puzzle...first circle eight well known girls names hidden in the grid. Then unscramble the remaining letters to reveal the title of a well-known song (five words).

When you have written the song title in the space provided below, don't forget to fill in your name and address, pop this page into an envelope (you don't need a stamp) and post it today! Hurry—competition ends 31st October 1996.

Mills & Boon Song Puzzle
FREEPOST
Croydon
Surrey
CR9 3WZ

Song Title: _____

Are you a Reader Service Subscriber?   Yes ❏   No ❏

Ms/Mrs/Miss/Mr _____

Address _____

_____

——————————— Postcode ———————

One application per household.

You may be mailed with other offers from other reputable companies as a result of this application. If you would prefer not to receive such offers, please tick box.   ❏

C396
D